PIERO VENTURA

HOUSES

Structures, Methods, and Ways of Living

With the Collaboration of
Max Casalini
Pierluigi Longo
Marisa Murgo Ventura

HOUGHTON MIFFLIN COMPANY

BOSTON 1993

CONTENTS

Copyright © 1992 by Arnoldo Mondadori Editore S.p.A.
English translation © 1993 Arnoldo Mondadori Editore S.p.A.
First American edition 1993
Originally published in Italy in 1992 by Mondadori
All rights reserved. For information about permission
to reproduce selections from this book, write to
Permissions, Houghton Mifflin Company,
215 Park Avenue South, New York, New York 10003.
Cataloging-in-Publication Data is available from the U.S. Library of Congress.
Printed in Italy by Arnoldo Mondadori - Verona
10 9 8 7 6 5 4 3 2 1

INTRODUCTION

We have always tried to change our environment to suit our needs; we have hunted for and found food, we have tried to protect ourselves from the dangers lurking there, we have protected our bodies with clothes that allowed us to work well in different climates (when, for example, the seasons changed and the weather turned cold), and we have tried to survive in the best way possible (sometimes even enjoying ourselves by finding or making beautiful things). We have also tried to defend ourselves against natural enemies, like the forces of nature. To fulfill this last need, we built houses, places in which to live where we could be protected; where families, the smallest social structure, could gather; and where we could also carry out certain activities. Our story is the story of our houses, of the ever-changing ways of satisfying the needs of protection and security, of ever-developing technology, and of continually changing styles that influenced the way houses were built.

Consider the relationship between people and stone as a building material. Thanks to its strength (it doesn't warp, and it can't be compressed) stone has always seemed the ideal material for making long-lasting objects. But although pebbles are abundant everywhere, it is not always easy to find large rocks that have the right shape for making what we want. If you gather some rocks on a beach and try to pile them up, you will soon realize that when rounded, they tend to roll away from where you want them, simply because of gravity. A piece of stone is very useful for construction if it is square or roughly cubed, but people learned quickly that the strength of stone posed a problem: it was hard to change its shape. For thousands of years man had tried to chip stones in order to make tools and weapons, but it was a different matter altogether to try to get an adequate block for construction just by chipping at a piece of rock. For this reason, the first real houses in Neolithic times were made not of stone, but of wood or reeds.

The discovery of ceramics, of the possibility of hardening clay by drying or heating it after giving it the required shape, offered a new and practical construction material with which we could make bricks—perfect for building houses. Only then could human beings, numerous and able to tackle even complex technical problems, go back to stone for building more important edifices than just simple houses. So in Egypt, Greece, and Rome (and even in the great American civilizations before Columbus discovered them) temples were built for gods, palaces and great tombs for kings, and places for carrying out public activities of interest to the whole community; in short, buildings that were destined to last forever.

CAVES

Cavemen never really lived in caves; they just used them for certain activities. Sometimes they used them for shelter, but more often they used them as resting places for the dead, for repairing tools, and for magic.

Caves must have seemed just as fascinating and mysterious to our distant ancestors as they do to us: frightening places where darkness hangs over everything. People entered caves only when they learned how to make torches; then they were able to work even during the night, driving away sleeping animals or frightening them with fire.

People were then able to inhabit the deepest parts of caves and use them for magic ceremonies. By drawing animals on the walls, they could conjure them up, and by striking the drawings with stones or spears, they could be sure that through magic they could catch the real animals during the hunt outside the cave. There are many examples of such cave wall art.

Near the entrance of the caves, men chipped at stones, especially flint, a rock similar to quartz and made mostly of silica (silicon dioxide). Working with systematic precision they could make sharp-edged instruments, used as knives or points for spears and arrows.

In the deepest parts of some caves people drew or painted animals, hunting tools, and less often hunters.

Chipped and pointed flint was used to kill and skin animals, cut the meat, and strip bark.

In most cases people did not live in caves the way we live in houses; they did only certain things there. Everyday life was led outside or in shelters below rocks.

Deepest cave area

Primary cave area

Stalactites

Supplies were kept in small crevices, perhaps to "feed" the dead.

Ground level

The dead were buried in shallow graves dug at ground level and then covered with leaves and flowers and often surrounded by ornaments or weapons.

Sometimes fragments of flint can be found at ground level, which are remnants of chipping, and traces of burned materials that are the remains of fires used to keep animals away and to cook meat.

PILE DWELLINGS

People in their environment experienced a big jump in the quality of life when ten to twelve thousand years ago our ancestors discovered that by heating clay they could obtain a very strong material known as terracotta or ceramic. It became possible not only to make bowls and vases, but also to plaster bunches of straw and mats to strengthen them.

In this era (a cultural period known as Neolithic), people discovered that by putting seeds in the earth (for example, barley and later wheat), they could grow new plants and seeds; they also discovered that by protecting certain animals (goats, sheep, and later cattle and geese) they could get useful products from them (milk, fur, horn, and meat), and they learned that animal and human excrement could help plants grow. Thus people went from being hunter-gatherers to farmer-breeders.

Communities gradually became more numerous. Huts were built close together in order to form villages. Although water is vital for agriculture and animal rearing, there are times when there can be too much water, such as with floods and high tides. For this reason large structures like platforms were built near lakes and lagoons which were detached from the water; sometimes they were several miles long and made with tree trunks and planks of wood (interesting remains can still be found north of Lake Garda, Italy).

Such structures or platforms allowed people to steal space from the water and build on it. In some cases, frequent floods or tidal movements forced people to raise the huts high above the water, placing them on top of shelves, called pile dwellings because the piles were stuck, or planted, into the bottom of the water. Such villages are still common in New Guinea and in some islands of Polynesia.

In these lake-dwelling settlements many-leveled structures are common; they are not houses with many floors, but rather storage areas like warehouses on large platforms. The presence of water all around the piles and under the lower floors stops mice from reaching stored food (especially grain).

Usually fires were kept lit outside the huts for safety.

Areas of shallow water near the lakeshore

Often canoes were made of one tree trunk hollowed out and waterproofed with clay. These canoes are called dugouts.

6

The huts had straw or reed walls covered in clay; the straw roofs were supported by beams.

The supporting poles were stuck deep into the muddy bottom.

The inhabitants of pile dwellings hunted aquatic birds with nets and arrows, gathered molluscs, and fished by using spears, fishing lines, and hooks.

Grain storage areas were usually built under the roof to keep the grain away from rats.

The house was kept cool by keeping the number of windows to a minimum, and fires were avoided by building furnaces on the balconies.

The columns that supported the attic through the various floors were made of wood; brick columns were used only in cellars.

The dry climate allowed people to construct dry and cool cellars that were very good at preserving food and handmade goods.

The walls, which were always plastered, were built with technically crude clay-and-straw bricks that had been dried in the sun.

To go from one story to another people usually used ladders; however, in this model of a rich official's house, you will see plastered-brick stairs, even on landings.

EGYPT

The Nile, which regularly overflows at certain seasons of the year, enriches the soil around it with a narrow band of fertile mud on both banks (consisting of rotting vegetable and animal substances) and carries clay downstream. Egyptian civilization developed very quickly because agricultural production was so abundant. The Egyptians had to build dikes, canals, and catch basins for water so that they could make the most of the river's production system. Not far from the river, the hills offered interesting construction materials: calcareous rocks, granites, and basalts. Wood was rather scarce (the only common tree was the palm tree), but rushes were abundant. The dry climate allowed the Egyptians to make clay objects simply by leaving them out in the sun to dry; for thousands of years Egyptian huts were built with crude bricks made in this way.

According to historical tradition, the first person to construct buildings "that would last forever" was Imhotep, around 2800 B.C.; we can therefore consider him history's first architect. Imhotep was in charge of the construction, in lime blocks, of the temple and the step pyramid of Sakkara (near Cairo) for King Zoser.

Although palaces, temples, and royal tombs were made of stone or dug out of rock, houses were still made of crude bricks, with small amounts of wood and reeds. When such buildings collapsed, others were built in exactly the same way, on top of the ruins of the first one.

The most elaborate houses, like the one illustrated, were owned by high-ranking officials and contained many floors; the simplest houses had only one floor, grain deposits, ovens, and small enclosures for poultry. There weren't many windows, and furniture was made of wood and reeds, sometimes of leather. All containers (vases, pitchers, cups) were made of clay fired in kilns (that is, ceramic) and were often painted. Blue glazed ceramic, made by melting copper salts on the surface, was very common, and amulets against curses were often in the shape of scarab beetles. Metal was used less often, mainly for making weapons and precious jewels.

A GREEK HOUSE

Many temples from ancient Greece have been preserved (partly because some were later turned into Christian churches, like the Temple of Concord in Agrigento, Sicily, and the Temple of Athena in Syracuse, whose columns are surrounded by a cathedral). They were built with stone.

Remains of houses are not as common, but there are many descriptions in literary texts. The best remains are those discovered at Olynthus; from the structure of these ruins we can see that the Greeks had a good system of urban planning. Even at the time of Athens' greatest splendor (sixth to fourth centuries B.C.), streets and districts were carefully arranged. Like in many other big cities, particular attention was paid to planning public areas, which had large squares (called *agora*) used for commercial activities and kept separate from workshops, houses, and the sacred ground (often placed on top of a hill, called *acropolis*, or "high city") where temples were built.

Descriptions and archaeological excavations (which have uncovered the remains of potteries and sculptors' workshops, as well as traces of ceramic pipes used for water distribution) help us reconstruct a typical Greek house of the fifth century B.C. The walls were made of brick or stone, the roofs of two kinds of tile: flat tiles (square with two raised sides) interlocked with bent tiles shaped like fingernails.

The Greek word for bricks, *plinthos,* goes back to a term from ancient Crete: the tradition of building with bricks must have been brought over to Greece from that great Mediterranean island with a powerful sea civilization (that is, based on commercial exchanges made by ship) which flourished two to three thousand years before Christ.

The house was divided into different areas where people worked on various crafts (there was, of course, always a kitchen and a larder), and there were other rooms where the inhabitants could rest. These rooms were arranged around a small square courtyard that might have been surrounded by columns of stone. In cities like Athens, which had many craftsmen, the availability of water in shops also provided citizens with good sanitation in homes.

From the fifth to the third century B.C. Athens and other cities in Greece (and in present-day Turkey, like Samos) had a flourishing ceramics industry, including the production of bricks and tiles.

Ovens were usually placed on shelves, under which bundles of sticks were kept.

Alongside the interior courtyard there could be a colonnade used as a secondary corridor.

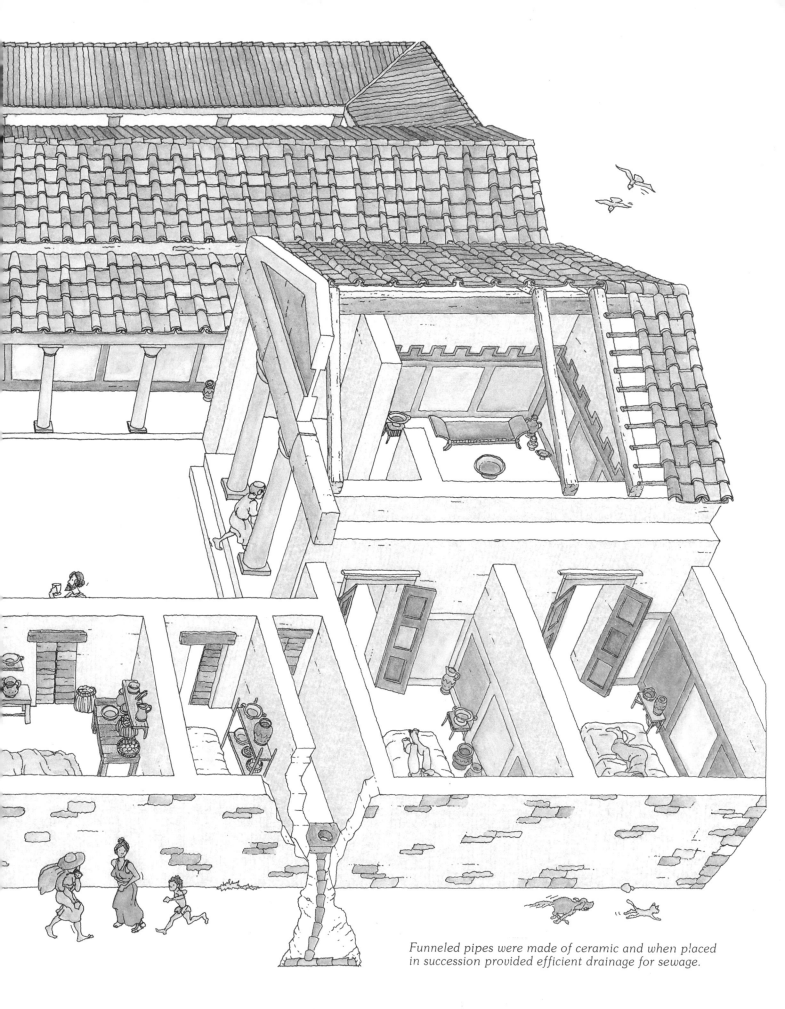

Funneled pipes were made of ceramic and when placed in succession provided efficient drainage for sewage.

BUILDING WITH STONE

Blocks of stone used in ancient times were often very big; there were various methods of extracting them from the quarry which would allow people to produce large square masses.

One common method was to plant wedges and chocks of wood in holes made in the rock, then force them to expand by pouring water on them. In this way the blocks would detach themselves from the rocky wall.

The problem of transporting these blocks was resolved differently in different places. Usually people used sledges; when near a river, the longest journeys were undertaken by raft.

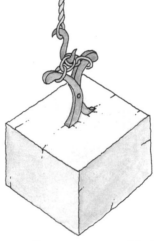

There were many ways of harnessing the blocks and lifting them; one was to dig U-shaped grooves on two opposite sides of the rock and then wedge in two loops of rope tied together on top.

Craftsmen could insert iron pieces in appropriate holes that were then turned to jam them inside, and wedged in to keep them in that position.

Two iron prongs like a pair of scissors could be inserted in opposite holes; when tightened by a chain at the top they would widen at the bottom, fixing themselves into the holes.

The gripping mechanism could be a pincer that, when tightened by a rope, would close into the two opposite holes made in the stone block.

The final positioning of the blocks was done by using wooden poles and wedges.

Place where the
rope was attached

There was
another
pulley here.

An important part of a
crane is the hoist, made
with a mobile pulley
with a rope around it.

The hoist

In the construction yards of imperial Rome, the
winch's axis was turned by a circular cage where one
or more men walked as if they were climbing stairs.

In order to lift the weight, the rope is wrapped
with the winch on a rotating cylinder called a
drum.

Ropes called braces kept
the two arms of the crane in
position.

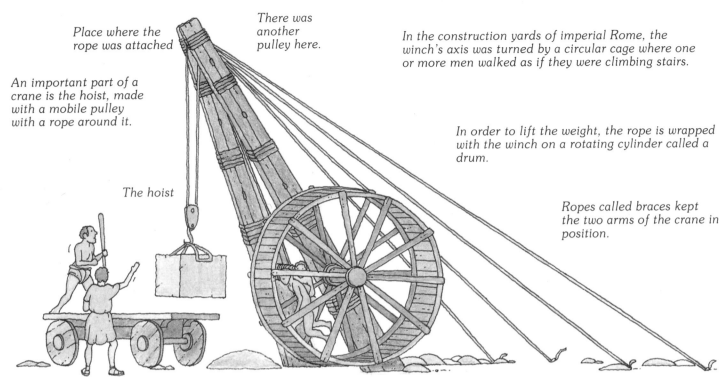

The machines and tools used in stone-construction yards hardly changed from the late Roman period to
the Middle Ages and even the early part of the Renaissance.

Chisels

Hammers

Many features of stone structures (like the drum or capital
of a column) had to be accurately carved before being used;
most important, the surfaces that were going to be joined
together had to be absolutely flat. Brushes and blades
combined with abrasive dust made by crumbling harder
kinds of stone were used to smooth the surfaces.

Walls made with stone blocks stay straight because of
gravity; the weight of each block on top of the others is
enough to keep the structure standing. The various
segments were linked together by pouring molten lead into
small holes made in the rock, making sure that eventual
shifts of the ground or fractures in the rock would not
destroy the unity of the building.

A ROMAN CITY HOUSE

The majority of architectural remains from the Roman civilization are also palaces, temples, villas, and structures of public interest such as bridges, aqueducts, baths and pools, roads and theaters. Although many houses were destroyed, we do have one very interesting example of houses that were preserved by a great natural disaster: the eruption of the volcano Vesuvius on August 24, A.D. 79; the eruption buried many flourishing cities near Naples with lava, ash, and mud. These cities were Pompeii, Herculaneum, Oplontis, and Stabiae. Because these cities were practically frozen in time at the height of their activity, the excavations there give us a good picture of everyday life. The largest city, Pompeii, consisted of many kinds of buildings: shops, workshops, eating places, houses with rooms to let, rich citizens' homes, villas (outside the city walls), and, of course, temples, public baths, gymnasiums, and theaters. Usually houses had brick walls, sometimes mixed with stone, and typically they had only one floor. The house of a well-to-do

A roof that slopes toward the atrium was sometimes supported by four columns.

Butcher's shop

Walls were decorated with encaustic painting (a process whereby the colors were mixed in hot wax and then applied to the plaster)

An inn

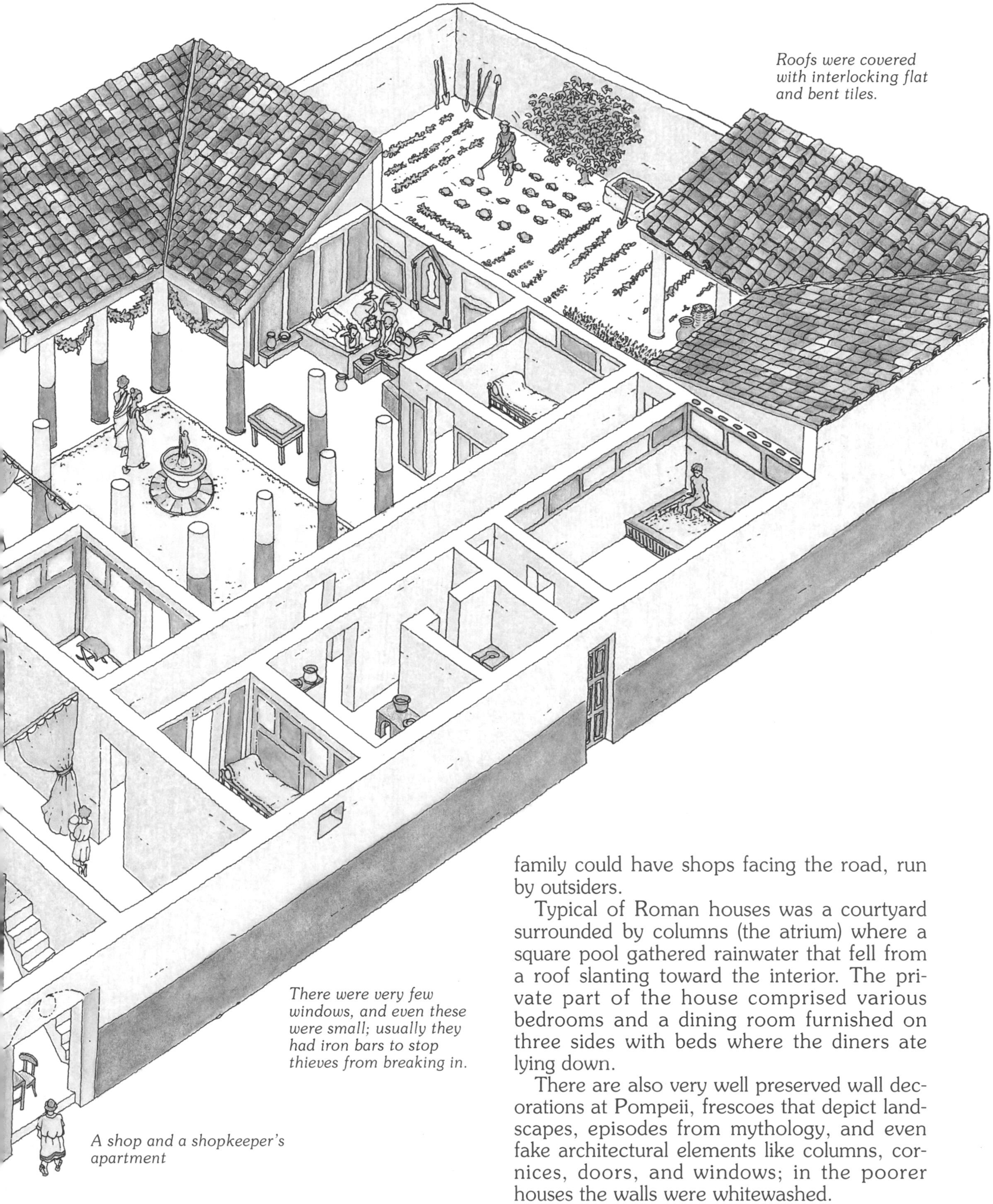

Roofs were covered
with interlocking flat
and bent tiles.

There were very few
windows, and even these
were small; usually they
had iron bars to stop
thieves from breaking in.

A shop and a shopkeeper's
apartment

family could have shops facing the road, run
by outsiders.

Typical of Roman houses was a courtyard
surrounded by columns (the atrium) where a
square pool gathered rainwater that fell from
a roof slanting toward the interior. The private part of the house comprised various
bedrooms and a dining room furnished on
three sides with beds where the diners ate
lying down.

There are also very well preserved wall decorations at Pompeii, frescoes that depict land-
scapes, episodes from mythology, and even
fake architectural elements like columns, cornices, doors, and windows; in the poorer
houses the walls were whitewashed.

THE ROMAN INSULA

Houses in big cities were different from the one-story homes of Pompeii and Herculaneum; usually they contained many apartments spread out over many floors (up to four or five). People did not live well in these houses; because of the number of inhabitants and the lack of running water (usually each family group took their daily water from a public fountain in the street and brought it inside), hygiene was poor. Also, there were no toilets in the houses. Spaces were narrow, ceilings were low, and stairs awkward. These housing developments could be very big, and when surrounded by four streets they were called *insulae* ("islands").

Obviously, such housing methods were

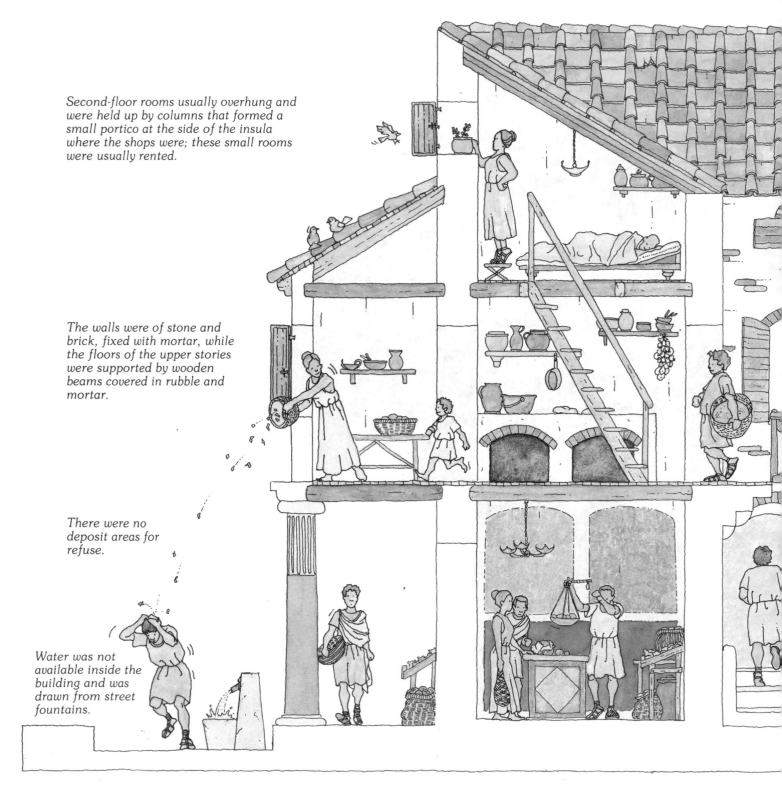

Second-floor rooms usually overhung and were held up by columns that formed a small portico at the side of the insula where the shops were; these small rooms were usually rented.

The walls were of stone and brick, fixed with mortar, while the floors of the upper stories were supported by wooden beams covered in rubble and mortar.

There were no deposit areas for refuse.

Water was not available inside the building and was drawn from street fountains.

adopted in big cities because, like today, space was precious and there were many citizens (1,200,000 in imperial Rome) who needed to live near their workplace. Among the best examples of surviving multistoried insulae are those at Ostia, a Roman port, where the progressive sinking of the ground has buried even very tall buildings.

The popular insula was built with bricks and secondhand materials. The strength of these constructions was mediocre, partly because of the many floors placed on top of each other; there is evidence that they sometimes collapsed, and many people were crushed. The cost of a lease was high, and a single room contained beds and cooking and heating implements, which often caused disastrous fires.

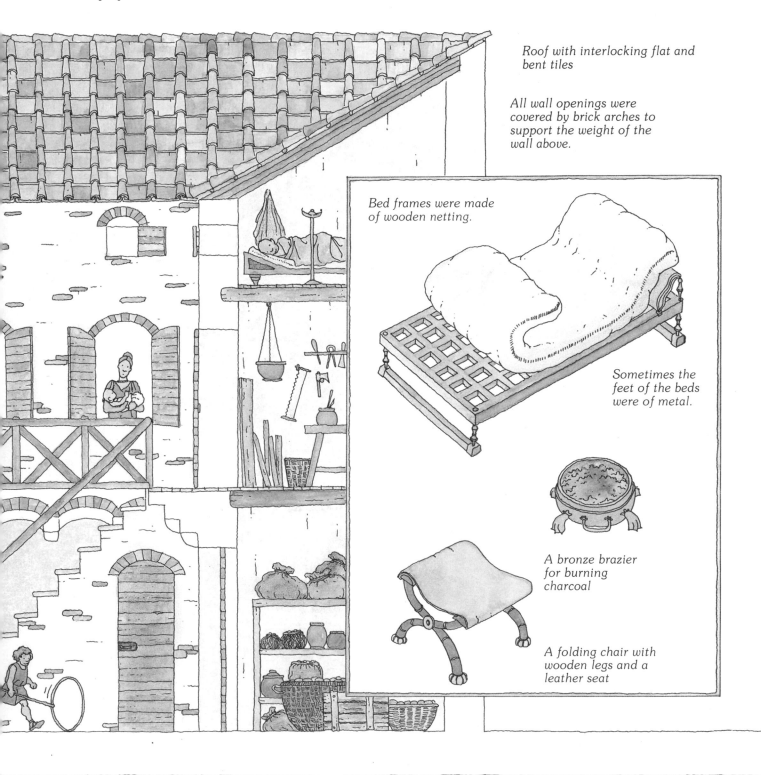

Roof with interlocking flat and bent tiles

All wall openings were covered by brick arches to support the weight of the wall above.

Bed frames were made of wooden netting.

Sometimes the feet of the beds were of metal.

A bronze brazier for burning charcoal

A folding chair with wooden legs and a leather seat

THE VIKINGS OF THE NORTH

What we know about the Vikings, great navigators who came from Scandinavia and invaded all of Europe between A.D. 700 and 1100, derives mainly from written legends in which the stories of their exploits were handed down to us. Feared by the people they attacked and considered uncivilized and bru-

Buildings were made with large tree trunks taken from the area and bound together with joints; wedges, pegs, and even iron and copper nails gave the whole greater strength.

The roof had a framework of wooden beams and rafters and was covered by wooden tiles.

In the outside walls there were small high windows made of wood.

The outline of the house was established by a series of large poles stuck in the ground; a second series of interior poles was a support for the roof.

tal, in reality the Vikings were sophisticated craftsmen especially skilled in metalwork. They crafted not only swords and shields, but also beautiful gold objects.

Archaeologists have tried to uncover the truth hidden in the ancient sagas, which tell of voyages across the sea to faraway lands, in particular toward Iceland and Greenland; references to even farther places are not uncommon. That is why there was a suspicion that the Vikings had reached North America at least four centuries before Columbus. By studying the routes that these texts describe, archaeologists in the 1960s discovered a settlement on the northern part of the island of Newfoundland, where many different buildings were found. An examination of the remains of this site, called L'Anse aux Meadows, ruled out the possibility of its being an Eskimo or Native American village, or even a seasonal base for whale hunters.

Certain objects (iron nails, fragments of copper, stone loom weights) are without doubt the products of Viking craftsmen and have been carbon-dated to A.D. 1000, the era that coincides with the voyages of Leif Ericson, the hero of Norwegian and Icelandic sagas. L'Anse aux Meadows could therefore be a Viking settlement.

Parts of the L'Anse aux Meadows site are an elliptical longhouse (twenty meters long), a forge for working iron, and a charcoal pile (a building where tree trunks were turned into charcoal, a substance used in metalworking).

Hollow horns were decorated and used for drinking; they were also used to make wind instruments for sending signals.

The interior was divided into many rooms by partitions.

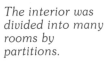

Beds had wooden jointed frames or metal nails.

Precious metal cups and basins were often embossed.

The mild climate allowed the large colonnaded terraces to be used as living areas for most of the year, with open lacunar ceilings that could be decorated in different ways.

Structural walls were made of brick; marble and stucco were used for decoration, and imaginative use was made of different colors. The structural components used to spread the weight of the upper walls were, as in imperial Roman architecture, the arches, usually made of large flat bricks in the shape of a fan.

Walls surrounded the city, and along two sides they fell to the sea; there were many towers for surveillance and for defense.

BYZANTIUM

In A.D. 330 Emperor Constantine gave the ancient city of Byzantium a new name, Constantinople, and made it the capital of the Roman Empire of the east. By changing its name and establishing it as his residence, Constantine wanted to demonstrate the importance of the east and contrast his Christian capital with the still pagan city of Rome, mainly for political reasons.

In time, Constantinople flourished and took back the name Byzantium. A cultural center where its Greek heritage mingled with Roman, eastern, and even Jewish traditions to support the new demands of Christianity (now the official state religion), Byzantium had magnificent public areas with space for the large hippodrome, the majestic cisterns of the imperial palace (two of which were underground), and the system of aqueducts. Then, in the sixth century, at the height of the city's development, Emperor Justinian had the church of Santa Sophia rebuilt. Its magnificence was the symbol of Byzantine splendor.

There were also, however, overcrowded districts with small houses and inadequate sanitation; in fact, most of the water went to sections of the imperial palace. The use of public baths, typical of Roman culture, was discouraged by Christian mores. The port, a source of wealth and a center for all kinds of commercial activity, exposed the city to the danger of epidemics.

Our reconstruction of private buildings owned by the richer citizens of Byzantium is based on a study of the few remains, on the descriptions in the abundant literature of the time, and on a comparison of such descriptions with well-preserved late-Roman buildings in other parts of the empire.

BUILDING WITH BRICKS

People quickly learned about the properties of clay; malleable and easily worked by hand, this material became hard (but fragile) if subjected to intense heat. Thus people started to make the first simple terracotta containers, which were slowly improved by turning the clay on a potter's wheel. Clay becomes fairly hard even when dried only in the sun, especially if the mixture is made stronger by adding vegetable matter such as straw.

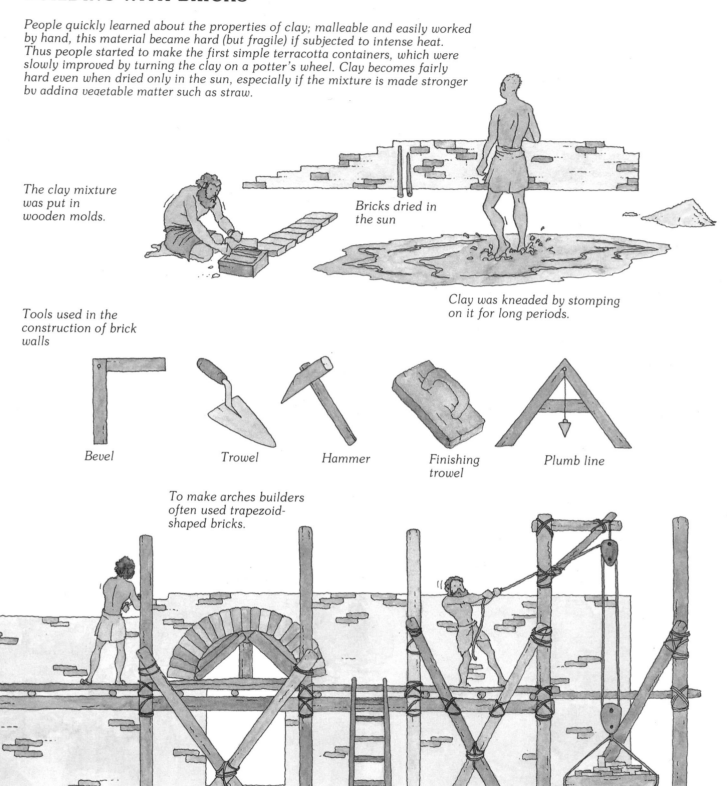

The clay mixture was put in wooden molds.

Bricks dried in the sun

Clay was kneaded by stomping on it for long periods.

Tools used in the construction of brick walls

Bevel

Trowel

Hammer

Finishing trowel

Plumb line

To make arches builders often used trapezoid-shaped bricks.

Kilns for firing lime were often underground, where heat was retained better.

Lime comes from cooking limestone; by placing the stone in hot, specially made ovens where airflow and oxygen can be controlled, one creates a material that contains mostly calcium oxide; this material is called caustic lime and can be made into slaked lime (or lime paste) by adding water; by mixing slaked lime with various quantities of sand, it becomes mortar, which is spread between bricks.

In this kind of kiln lime and bricks could be fired at the same time.

A hoe, a tool with a flat spade and a long handle, was used to stir the mixture.

Ceramic (or terracotta) amphorae were used for carrying water.

A complex mechanism inside the castle allowed inhabitants to raise the drawbridge to stop unwanted visitors from gaining access by the main gate.

Fireplaces were usually only in the largest halls, kept mainly for social occasions, and in the kitchens; bedrooms did not have fireplaces.

Chimneys and smoke vents were inside the thick walls.

There was a walkway made mostly of wood at the top of the encircling walls for the guards; overhanging the edge, these covered corridors were called bartizans. On the floor of the bartizan were holes that allowed the besieged to throw objects on attackers.

CASTLES

Castles were built because the feudal lord promised to protect his vassals from enemy attack in exchange for their labor. Therefore castles usually had to include areas for supplies, armories, stables, wells, and cisterns; they also had to be built in places where an enemy's approach could be seen in time to organize an efficient defense in case of siege.

There are castles all over Europe, and the oldest ones date from just before A.D. 1000. They were built with a first enclosure of walls, inside which were one or more courtyards; inside these was the keep, a fortified tower offering shelter to the inhabitants, which in time became a sought-after dwelling.

The towers and external walls presented a sloping base; the larger girth of the massive walls in the lower regions of the castle gave it greater strength. An attacker's task was made more difficult because the inclined walls allowed the besieged to throw all kinds of objects on the attackers, including boiling water and oil.

Interior constructions like floors and stairs were made of wood; because of the size of the rooms, pillars of stone, wood, and less often brick were sometimes necessary to support the upper levels. To cover the larger rooms, vaulted roofs were used, just like in churches.

TOWERS

The medieval city, surrounded by walls, duplicated and expanded the layout of the castle. Many houses were built close together, and shops, workshops, and warehouses were added once commercial and craft activities in the twelfth and thirteenth centuries had begun to revive. Roads were narrow and, of course, tall buildings made better use of the limited space. Towers might initially

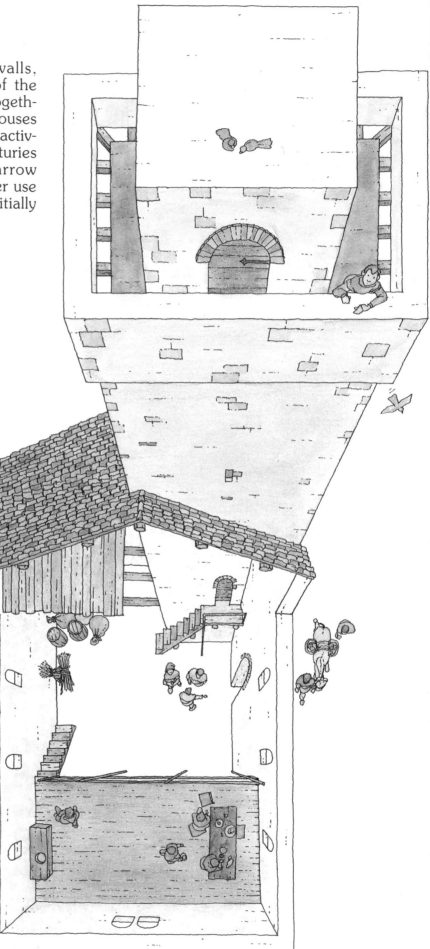

From the outside, towers look rather severe; but inside they could be furnished to cater to all the requirements of the inhabitants. The walls were often painted and the use of drapes or carpets as temporary partitions was common.

The roofs, which were slightly inclined, were covered with tiles, often just interlocking mound shapes placed right-side up and upside-down to make a joint.

All the floors and partitions in the building were made of thick planks of wood that leaned against the beams.

Buildings were made of stone to make them stronger; inside, the floors, stairs, and the few partition walls were of wood.

In the courtyard, a platform was used as a rest area for the servants; the area underneath was used as a simple shelter for goods before they were assigned to other storage areas.

26

have had some strategic importance; soon, however, they became a symbol above all of social importance. A high tower represented the prestige and power of the family who lived there. Many Italian cities that flourished as communes in the Middle Ages, such as San Gimignano and Tarquinia, are even today like forests of high stone towers. There are also tower houses, where the tower is only the highest part of a building extended with various small sections and courtyards. Towers were wider at the top,

where there was a kind of terrace surrounded by a wall. This wall overhung the rest of the building and was supported by a series of brackets or small arches called corbels. Because of the widespread use of wood in interior construction (floors, stairs, and walls), fires were common. However, the outer stone walls were seldom damaged; in many ruined towers today you can still see traces of rooms, marked on the walls by the holes where large support beams used to hold up the floors.

The overhanging upper part of the tower was supported by a series of shelves called corbels.

The windows were very small and had wooden frames; the shutters were of solid wood.

A HOUSE IN THE LATE MIDDLE AGES

After 1300, cities developed everywhere: at the crossroads of frequently used roads, in high places where it was easy to dominate the surrounding countryside, and near mineral sources or salt marshes. They were always encircled by walls with gates.

Inside the walls space was limited, and it was always necessary to build upward. Merchants' houses in particular combined living areas, storage areas, and a shop in which to sell goods. Craftsmen's houses also

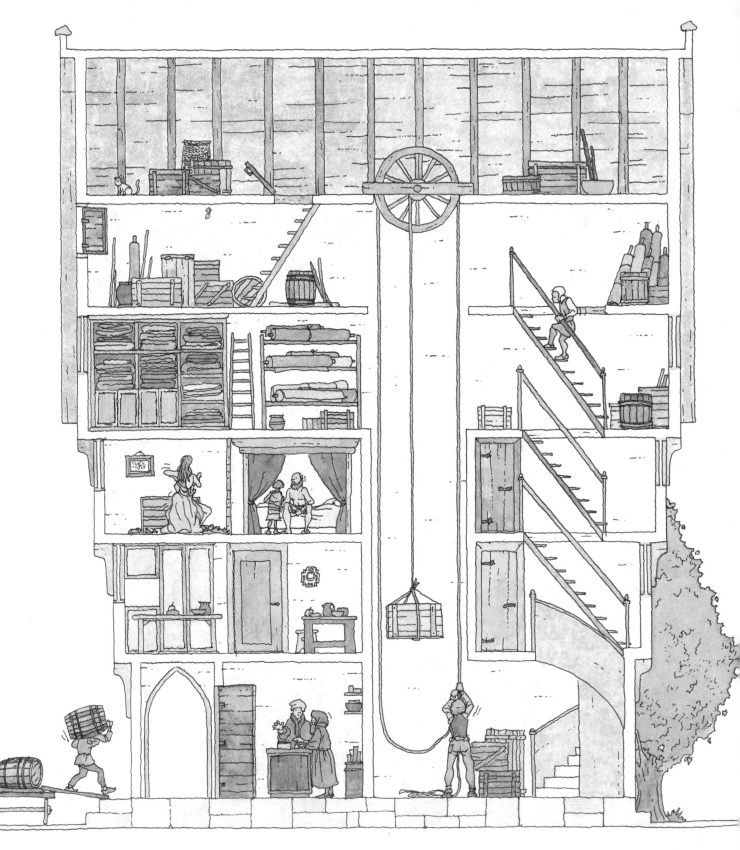

included areas set aside as workshops.

The prosperity of these towns was proportionate to the ever-increasing wealth of a new social class that derived its riches from the exchange of manufactured and partly manufactured goods; it also became useful to be able to loan money, hence the emergence of what were basically usurers and bankers. As a whole this social class would take its name from the word *bourg,* medieval town, and would be called the bourgeoisie.

For practical reasons connected with commercial activity, the structure of the medieval city did not change until the 1400s. Houses still took up the same amount of space; they were extended by adding more floors, and sometimes the use of different rooms changed.

House styles varied from region to region; our illustration depicts a house in central Europe, with storage areas and a shop. The steeply inclined roof was typical of the area because of heavy snowfalls, and upper stories were used for the storage of goods. In Mediterranean regions, storage areas were usually on the ground floor.

The steeply sloping roof usually began on the third floor.

The brick walls did not have a load-bearing purpose, because the real frame of the house was made of the large tree trunks that were visible on the façade.

Hoists that extended from the first floor up to the highest point under the roof were used to lift heavy objects. Shops were open on the first floor, above which were living areas. Storage areas for salable goods, food, and tools were on the top floor.

Pointed arches were common, typical of Gothic style and frequently used in building the large cathedrals of the late Middle Ages.

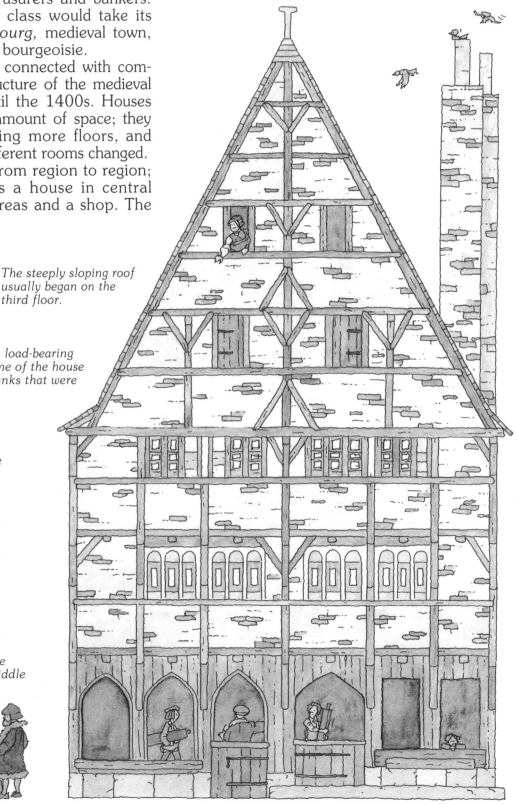

BUILDING WITH WOOD

*In the buildings of the past, wood was used mostly for constructing the floor and roof supports. Like in many medieval European city houses, the visible beams were part of the building's framework, whereas bricks, inserted into the framework, made up the walls. An essential part of the roof support was the truss, a kind of large **A** that gave the roof its shape, which sloped more or less steeply depending on where it was built.*

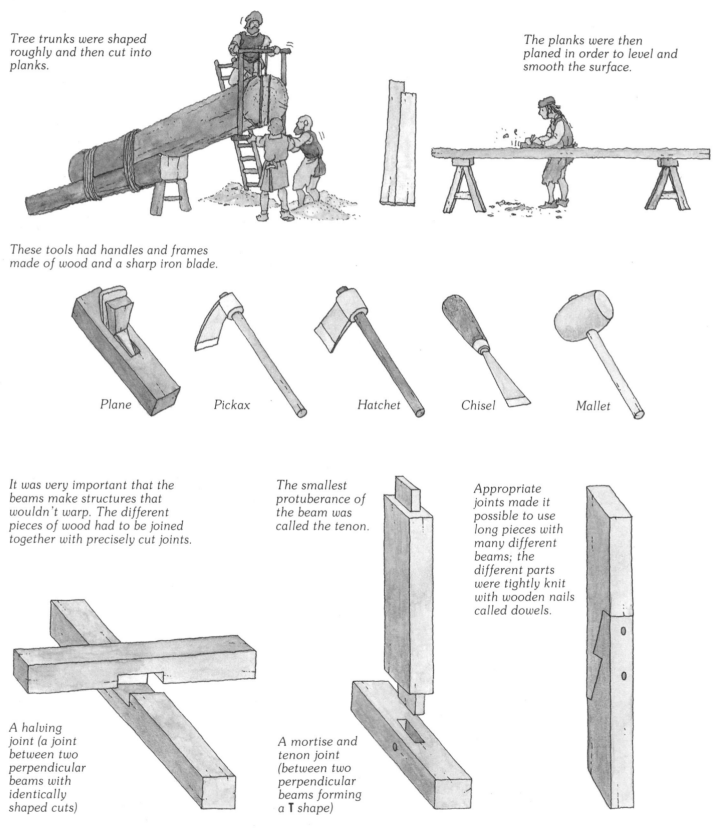

Tree trunks were shaped roughly and then cut into planks.

The planks were then planed in order to level and smooth the surface.

These tools had handles and frames made of wood and a sharp iron blade.

Plane   Pickax   Hatchet   Chisel   Mallet

It was very important that the beams make structures that wouldn't warp. The different pieces of wood had to be joined together with precisely cut joints.

The smallest protuberance of the beam was called the tenon.

Appropriate joints made it possible to use long pieces with many different beams; the different parts were tightly knit with wooden nails called dowels.

A halving joint (a joint between two perpendicular beams with identically shaped cuts)

*A mortise and tenon joint (between two perpendicular beams forming a **T** shape)*

30

Joiners specializing in construction woodwork are called carpenters; many special tools are used in woodwork.

Carpenters used hatchets to hew the beams roughly.

Before putting together the pieces for a truss, the joints were checked.

Wooden frame of a German house dating from the end of the 1500s; it is not very different from the houses of the late Middle Ages, because carpentry techniques did not change over time.

A temporary beam held a pulley used for lifting the various construction pieces.

Different parts, placed diagonally, held the trusses in place and strengthened the whole structure.

Since wood is ideal for its resistance to compression, its strength, and its flexibility, carpenters could make brackets to support overhanging floors.

A FARMHOUSE

Farmhouses have not changed much over the years; in the European countryside you can still come across buildings that were built four centuries ago.

Until about forty years ago, the rooms on the first floor of the main building were used as stables for large animals (cattle, donkeys) and as storage areas for wine, oil, and other farm products. The upper floor, which was reached by outside steps, contained the kitchen, a large fireplace, and near it the bedrooms. Usually these areas were covered by a roof with visible beams because there was no attic. The second floor was supported by beams and rafters and covered with clay blocks similar to flat bricks or tiles.

Windows with wooden frames and small glass windowpanes

In warm and dry places like kitchens, perishable foods such as cured meats were hung from the beams.

The fireplace in the main room on the second floor was used as a kitchen; the heat it produced warmed the nearby bedroom through a partition wall.

THE VILLAS OF PALLADIO

The buildings completed in the late 1500s by Andrea Palladio on the Venetian mainland are monuments of the late Renaissance, but they are also the starting point for new and important developments in the history of building styles. In his villas, Palladio set out to combine the separate functions of a country farm with a residence for landowners (*villa* comes from the Latin word for "farm"). Usually these buildings have two side wings used for storing farming machinery and produce, but also for the workers' use. These storage rooms are placed symmetrically in relation to the main structure, which is higher and more impressive and is usually reached by steps. The central block has a façade with a colonnade topped by a triangular tympanum. It is easy to see that Palladio was not only consciously imitating the models of the great classical buildings of Greece and Rome, but also reviving them, making them useful and practical for new purposes, always attentive to the relationship between the building and the environment and never forgetting the practical function of the building. Features of Palladian buildings became typical of a whole architectural style (called neoclassicism) that would become popular 150 years later, in the 1700s.

The interior of La Rotonda was decorated after the completion of the villa. The doors that opened onto the main hall led to the stairwells, placed so that they changed the circular shape of the hall to that of the square exterior. These hidden stairways led to the rooms on the upper floor. A balustrade of columns ran right around the main hall.

The functional parts of the building (storage rooms and living quarters for the peasants) were invisible; they were on the first floor, usually under the main hall, under the colonnades and partly under the stairs.

In the drawing, the upper part of the villa has been detached from the lower half to show the layout of the first floor.

The Palladian villa known as La Rotonda was built expressly as a kind of suburban pleasure palace: the entire structure surrounds the central main hall, which is topped by a cupola that provides light.

Like all roofs, the cupola was covered with tiles and was topped by a small lantern that provided light for the main hall.

Andrea Palladio's most famous villa, known as La Rotonda, is located on a hill near Vicenza, Italy. It has no side wings and is, instead, composed of a single vast circular hall that occupies the center of the building and is topped by a cupola; on its four sides are identical façades with stairs and colonnades. This simple structure perfectly satisfied the wishes of the man for whom it was made (a wealthy clergyman of the Capra family), since he wanted a place for entertainment and rest only.

LIVING IN VENICE

Venice is one of the few large Italian cities that cannot boast of a Roman heritage. The first buildings date from the middle of the fifth century A.D., when, as legend has it, groups of refugees escaping from barbarian invaders found shelter on the islands of the Venetian lagoon.

People built first on the islands of the lagoon, islands made of debris brought downstream and prone to sinking. In most cases it was necessary to support the soil with beams and rocks. This method was used systematically when the settlement grew. The shallow water was filled with rubble or square blocks, which were then secured by placing on them thick wooden beams stuck in the silt. Venetians were then able to construct artificial islands where they could build with traditional techniques.

The drawing on the opposite page has been simplified. Although it is obvious that Venetian houses had no underground basements, they did have, between the beams stuck in the mud and the first floor, foundations made of blocks of rock that were sometimes alternated with clay filling. The technical problem was not easily solved, because a house without a solid foundation is not very stable, and the weight of a building on a silted riverbed can cause it to sink completely.

In time, Venice became a city artificially built on water; the streets are canals and between streets are little alleyways called *calli* and small squares called *campielli,* often with

Large wall areas were usually decorated with frescoes, or more often with oil paintings. The sumptuous glass chandeliers were always made in the glassworks of Murano, an island in the lagoon.

a well in the middle. Pedestrians walk on footpaths along the canals, which are crossed by bridges.

In what was once the republic of Venice, a rich and powerful nation thanks to its commerce with the east, the architecture gives the impression of uniformity, even though the buildings date from different eras and are inspired by different styles.

Apart from the first floor, Venetian houses usually had two stories; there was always an attic. The stairs between floors were made of stone. Wood was extensively used for floorboards and ceiling decorations, always enriched with stucco (made of paste and plaster). Buildings were well lit with many large glass-paned windows. Canal water entered the house lobby to allow gondolas to reach the front door in shelter. The chimney tops had a particular shape—the outlet was sloped and sometimes even adjustable to make the chimneys more efficient when the direction of the wind changed.

A SMALL CHATEAU

The small castles found in many parts of France were built with a purpose very different from the late-Renaissance Palladian villas; they rarely combined with farming areas for agricultural production. Instead they were often surrounded by gardens that bordered onto cultivated land or woods where people went hunting for pleasure.

In the appearance of these buildings you can see the contributions of different architectural times and places: large windows already present in the residences of the Renaissance aristocracy, many columns and façades with tympana (like Palladian villas), steeply sloping roofs, and very high chimneys similar to those of medieval cities.

The dominant European architectural style of the 1600s and the first half of the 1700s was baroque. Baroque buildings seem to want to hide their straight vertical lines with

their swirling appearance, their decorations, their spirals and scrolls. Often baroque buildings such as churches and palaces seem excessive in their surface movement and completely reliant on visual effects (for example, Bernini's colonnade in Saint Peter's Square in Rome). It is worth remembering that the term "baroque" was originally the name for an irregularly shaped pearl, so the word really means "bizarre" or "unequal."

In the small French castles, built mostly in the 1600s and 1700s, baroque is especially evident in the interior decoration, whereas the fundamental lines of the building are more sober, also because foremost in the architect's mind was the building as a place in which to live. A typical example, from which this illustration was taken, is the Chateau Maisons-Laffitte, near Paris, built between 1642 and 1648 by François

Mansart, who also worked for the French court. Many other buildings are imitations of this castle and look like miniature royal palaces. The layout of the rooms (usually on two floors, with one or two garrets under the roof, known as "mansard roofs") is similar to an apartment with many rooms; the largest room is usually the entrance hall, which leads to other first-floor rooms and stairways.

Roofs were usually covered in slate. The architect Mansart lent his name to sloping roofs and to garrets with opening windows that ventilate and illuminate; generally speaking, these windows are also called mansards. First-floor and second-floor areas have large windows with many glass panes. The mansard roofs were usually used by the servants. Thanks to their well-planned interiors, many small chateaus in the French countryside are still used as private luxury villas.

Typical of French gardens were low-trimmed geometrically shaped hedges.

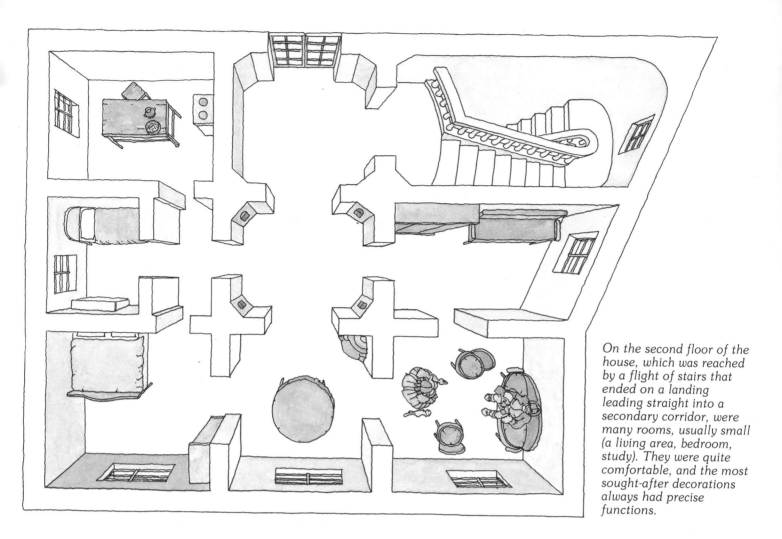

On the second floor of the house, which was reached by a flight of stairs that ended on a landing leading straight into a secondary corridor, were many rooms, usually small (a living area, bedroom, study). They were quite comfortable, and the most sought-after decorations always had precise functions.

AN EIGHTEENTH-CENTURY HOUSE IN PRAGUE

Churches, royal palaces, and public monuments, like art academies and libraries, are usually given as examples of the architectural style that followed the Renaissance; in such important baroque and rococo buildings (an eighteenth-century architectural movement that took over from baroque) the many curved features and rich decorations are witness to the technical skills of the architects and their innovative genius.

If, however, you look at the houses of merchants and artisans, you will see that these had the same basic structure in the 1600s as they did in the Middle Ages and the Renaissance. Only later, with the advent of the Enlightenment (a movement that emphasized the use of reason) did architects seem to address the fundamental but simple problem of satisfying the practical needs of people living in houses. And they did try to satisfy them in new and rational ways; they built small but well-lit and ventilated rooms with passages and hallways that gave easier access to different areas.

The internal layout of an eighteenth-century house in Bohemia, like the one illustrated, consisted of an entrance hall on the first floor (where small carriages could be kept), a kitchen, storage rooms, and servants' quarters; the rooms on the second floor made up a small apartment.

It is interesting to note that in this period porcelain was commonly used for making sought-after decorations, and also for making light, strong china, which was easy to clean, practical, and hygienic. Self-enclosed stoves replaced fireplaces and, since they weren't always placed against a wall, heat could circulate better throughout the house.

In the 1700s porcelain production became popular (the first producers of porcelain in Europe were in Meissen, Saxony, but soon after Italian manufacturers at Doccia and Capodimonte and French manufacturers in Sevres began producing it); porcelain is a very hard, white ceramic that contains kaolin, quartz, and feldspar.

Berlin ceramic

Porcelain dinner sets consisted of different objects used for different purposes: coffeepots, teapots, milk cups, sugar bowls, cups and coffee cups, saucers, soup plates and dinner plates, sauceboats, soup bowls, vegetable plates, and dishes. The wooden frames for mirrors were also decorated with porcelain features, as were large ovens.

FROM THE *ENCYCLOPÉDIE* TO THE REVOLUTION

Reacting to the excesses of baroque and rococo, the architects of the eighteenth century returned to the sober classicism of Palladio and even applied it to houses, which were built to satisfy the needs of the emerging and wealthy bourgeoisie that was now using homes as a status symbol. Large buildings that were groups of self-contained homes were constructed, similar to modern apartment buildings.

Roofs were covered with slate. Overhanging balconies were rare; instead windows often were as large as doors in order to let in more light and air and had a flat balcony railing.

The kitchen area was relatively small; the fireplace was often replaced with a brickwork cooker with a stove on top and a small closed oven underneath.

There were fireplaces in the living rooms and bedrooms; they all had their own chimneys, and on the roof the many chimney tops were grouped together. In rooms without fireplaces and in the bathrooms portable braziers were used.

The first examples worth noting were built in the city of Bath, England, around 1750, and later in London.

The layout of the interior reflected the needs of the owners and lodgers; the building was sometimes divided into parts, each with a different owner. Usually the owners of the building lived in the second-floor apartments, which were moderately ostentatious; these owners financed the construction of the building with money coming in from country rents or money often invested in commercial, industrial, or manufacturing businesses. On the upper stories or in the garrets lived middle-class lodgers, civil servants, or people working in the cultural sector (students and researchers, what we'd call intellectuals).

Toward the end of the eighteenth century, in all of Europe's capitals, and especially in London and Paris, the streets were lined with three- or four-storied buildings with sober façades and climbing colonnades resting on or semi-incorporated into the walls (pilasters) and with simple cornices for the many windows. Usually windows were smaller on the upper stories. In Paris in particular mansard roofs were common.

The bourgeoisie, represented so well by these houses, did not accept the fact that it was excluded from politics and supported initiatives started by intellectuals. Between 1751 and 1777 Diderot and d'Alembert published their famous *Encyclopédie*, where much space was dedicated to a description of people's work, their dignity as workers, and specific suggestions for the best ways to build houses in order to make them functional and practical.

The intellectuals, calling upon reason and the rights of man, denounced social inequalities, and in France the bourgeoisie financed a revolution that in 1789 caused the collapse of the old absolutist regime. Fifteen years earlier England had already lost through revolution its American colonies, which had proclaimed themselves an independent state.

On the eve of the French Revolution, the Parisian apartment of a professional or an intellectual comprised a kitchen, study, living room, and bedroom. There was also a bathroom, which did not have its own water supply.

In the French baroque and rococo periods, the many different architectural styles (mirrored in furniture such as chairs, tables, frames, mirrors, and lampshades) are named after the king of the time: Louis XIV, Louis XV, and Louis XVI.

Wall chandelier

Thanks to the painter Jacques-Louis David, Jean Paul Marat's bath is very famous. These bathtubs did not have drains and had to be filled and emptied with buckets.

Bathtubs were not common; we know that Marat used them often because he had a skin disease.

In the English working-class villages of the mid-1800s, houses were packed close together on very narrow, dark streets. The smoke from the factories, not far from these slums, mixed with the smoke from the chimneys, dimmed the light, and blackened the walls.

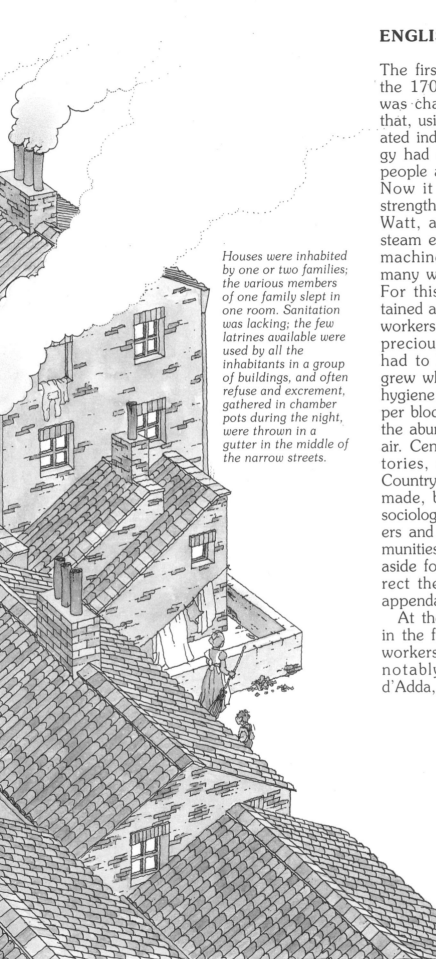

Houses were inhabited by one or two families; the various members of one family slept in one room. Sanitation was lacking; the few latrines available were used by all the inhabitants in a group of buildings, and often refuse and excrement, gathered in chamber pots during the night, were thrown in a gutter in the middle of the narrow streets.

ENGLISH SLUMS

The first industrial revolution took place in the 1700s. This important phase in history was characterized by the use of machines that, using combustible energy like coal, created industrial production. In the past, energy had come from the physical strength of people and animals, or from water or wind. Now it was replaced by the mechanical strength of steam engines, invented by James Watt, and factories were transformed. A steam engine could be connected to several machines, like spinning wheels, and thus many workers congregated in a small area. For this reason manufacturing areas contained a large concentration of people (many workers were also needed to mine the now precious coal). Workers and their families had to live close to the factories; villages grew where there was very little space and hygiene was poor (there was only one latrine per block). The situation was made worse by the abundance of smoke in the usually foggy air. Central England, with its mines and factories, soon became known as the Black Country. In the 1800s no improvements were made, but in the France of the mid-1800s sociologists and entrepreneurs supplied workers and their families with dwellings or communities called phalansteries, with space set aside for social activities in an effort to correct the alienating effect of their work as appendages to machines.

At the end of the nineteenth century and in the first decades of the twentieth century workers' villages were constructed in Italy, notably at Schio near Vicenza, Crespi d'Adda, and Turin (Leumann village).

Roofs were made of bent tiles. The narrow and squalid courtyards could not be used as vegetable patches because of the lack of light.

A MIDDLE-CLASS APARTMENT IN THE 1800S

In the second half of the nineteenth century many European cities were renovated through new urban planning. Old districts were demol-

Furniture was often exquisite and by the end of the century was made to imitate styles of the past.

Buildings often had a series of halls set aside as shops on the first floor, with many glass doors surrounded by arches; above these were three or four stories with an attic that could sometimes have dormer or mansard windows.

ished and large straight avenues appeared, giving new buildings space and with the strategic purpose of being too big to allow barricades to be set up during rebellions.

A rich middle-class apartment contained many rooms; there was always an entrance hall and a public area including the dining room and living room. Another part of the apartment, usually near the kitchen, was set aside for the servants. Many rooms were reserved for rest and personal affairs, including bedrooms and bathrooms; these now had taps connected to pipes hidden in the walls, as did the kitchen sink, put there during construction. In many cases hot water was available, provided by wood-burning water heaters. Among other sanitary objects there now was a toilet.

Lighting was gas-powered until the last years of the century. A public service was in charge of the distribution of gas (stoves still burned coal or wood). Later electric lighting was introduced and, at the same time, buildings were supplied with elevators that moved in complex metal frameworks inserted in the first floor or housed in the stairwell.

Balconies were an architectural feature that was already present in the buildings of the past; in nineteenth-century houses balconies were usually decorated with small cement columns.

There were always side staircases for suppliers which led directly to the servants' quarters.

Before our century, bidets with drains and taps were rare, whereas simple tubs were already in use.

Electric lighting was first used in ground-floor shops; the late-nineteenth-century advertisements for the bigger shops often featured the line "brightly lit."

HEATING HOUSES

A building is really useful to people if it offers the most appropriate environmental conditions for their activities; it is very important that the building be properly heated when it is cold outside and that the house be cool when the heat outside is unbearable. In the past it was enough to thicken walls to keep a place cool. Today our thin walls cannot function in that way anymore, and that is why we use air conditioners.

The history of heating is more interesting. In huts, the fire upon which people placed food to cook also provided necessary heat; until recently this was still true in farmhouses, where the fireplace was used for cooking and heating. The Romans in their public baths perfected a system of heating water with hot air (called a hypocaust, meaning "burning underneath"); the hot air created in specially made furnaces was circulated in gaps between bricks placed under the floors. In the seventeenth and eighteenth centuries, stoves made of fireproof materials or cast iron came into use.

The operating principle in heating systems of the second half of the nineteenth century was different: a furnace heated water in a boiler; when the water expanded because of the increase in temperature, it rose through pipes placed in various parts of the building and circulated through custom-built metal radiators that spread the heat throughout the area. When the water became cold and condensed, it descended through other pipes and returned to the boiler. This is the principle of central heating. The water was usually heated by burning coal.

Today gas burners are used, and because of the height of buildings pumps are needed to help the water circulate. The bigger the heated surface of the radiator the more efficient it is; that's why radiators have similar shapes and are made of similar materials.

The boiler was kept in the cellar; charcoal was poured into it through a special opening that faced the street or, more often, an internal courtyard.

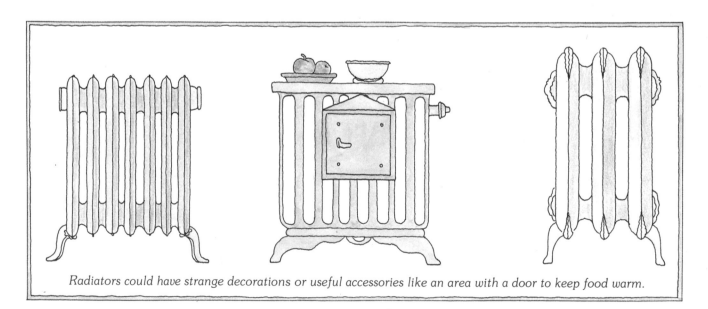

Radiators could have strange decorations or useful accessories like an area with a door to keep food warm.

Radiators for central heating, made of cast iron, were made of different parts connected by a conduit at the top and the bottom, allowing hot water to circulate.

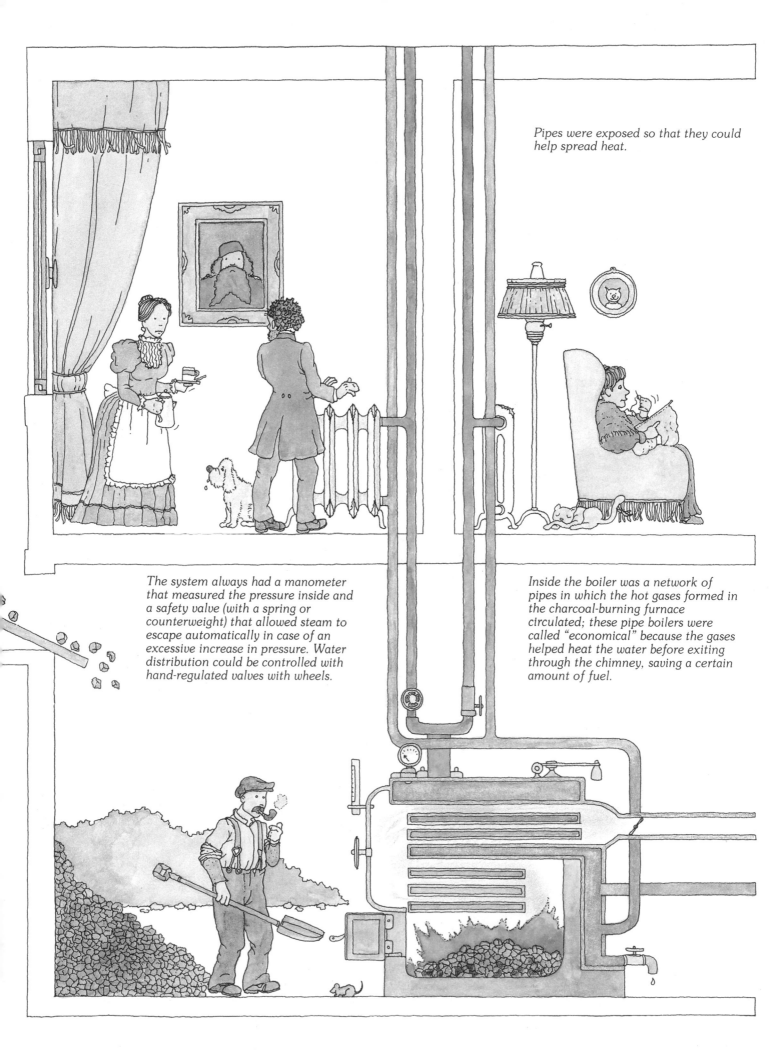

Pipes were exposed so that they could help spread heat.

The system always had a manometer that measured the pressure inside and a safety valve (with a spring or counterweight) that allowed steam to escape automatically in case of an excessive increase in pressure. Water distribution could be controlled with hand-regulated valves with wheels.

Inside the boiler was a network of pipes in which the hot gases formed in the charcoal-burning furnace circulated; these pipe boilers were called "economical" because the gases helped heat the water before exiting through the chimney, saving a certain amount of fuel.

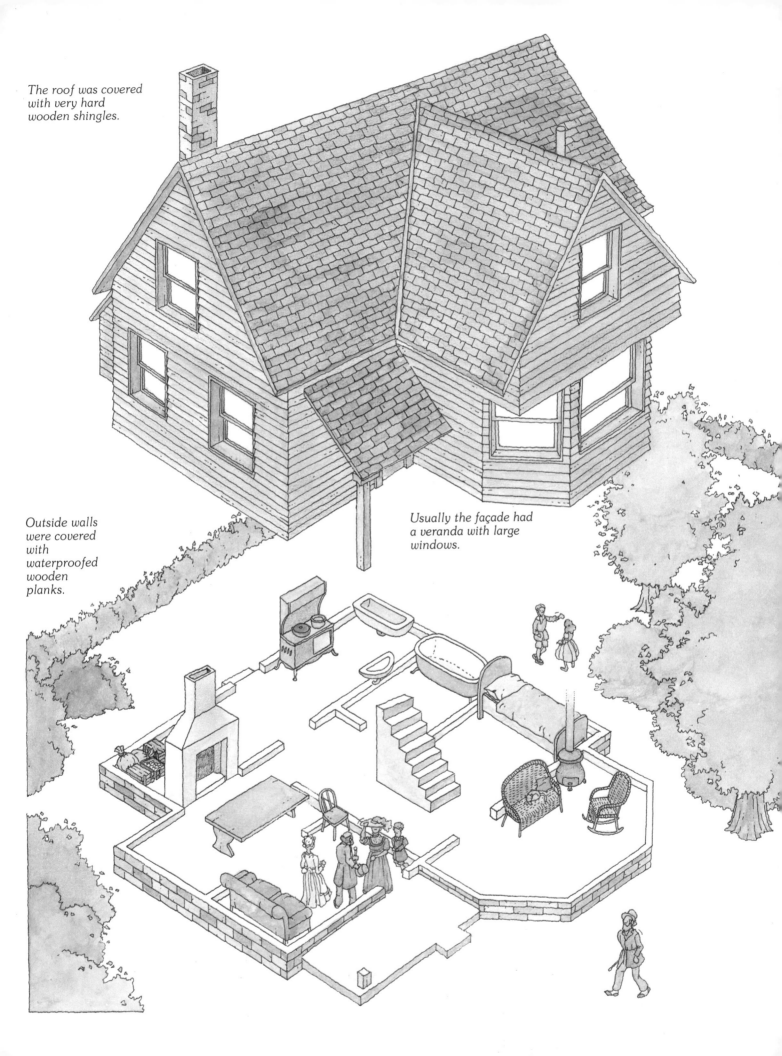

The roof was covered with very hard wooden shingles.

Outside walls were covered with waterproofed wooden planks.

Usually the façade had a veranda with large windows.

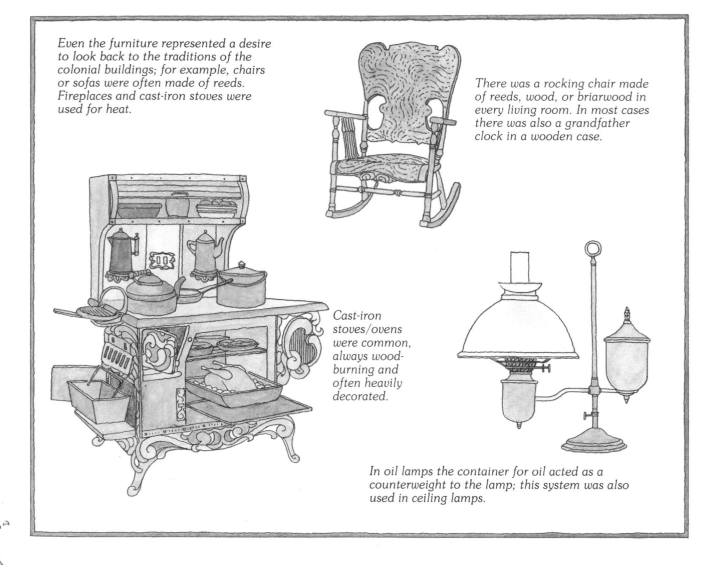

Even the furniture represented a desire to look back to the traditions of the colonial buildings; for example, chairs or sofas were often made of reeds. Fireplaces and cast-iron stoves were used for heat.

There was a rocking chair made of reeds, wood, or briarwood in every living room. In most cases there was also a grandfather clock in a wooden case.

Cast-iron stoves/ovens were common, always wood-burning and often heavily decorated.

In oil lamps the container for oil acted as a counterweight to the lamp; this system was also used in ceiling lamps.

THE AMERICAN FAMILY HOUSE

When you look at how much happened in the United States in the 1800s (especially the second half of the century), it is surprising to note that housing maintained its pioneer tradition. Buildings were constructed on large open spaces and with many autonomous parts, because there was no need to demolish old buildings to construct new ones as in Europe. These residential areas of small family homes were usually well linked with industrial and commercial centers via private and many efficient means of public transport.

Usually these houses consist of a first floor with a living room, kitchen, and sometimes bathroom and of a second floor with bedrooms that have angled ceilings because they occupy the garret area; load-bearing pillars form the structure, and the walls are covered with wooden planks. Only the base is made of brick. The floors are always wooden, and there is a brick-walled basement, dug out of the underlying earth. Heating was provided by cast-iron stoves (the traditional model was invented by Benjamin Franklin), with a fireplace usually in the living room. A wood-burning stove in the kitchen was also used.

Not all dwellings were this pleasant, especially near industrial centers, where many families responded to the need for large numbers of factory workers. Thus even in the U.S.A. slums similar to those in England appeared.

GROPIUS AND BAUHAUS

A fundamental phase in the history of art in our century, and particularly in the development of urban construction and planning, was what happened in Dessau, Germany, from 1919 onward. There the architect Walter Gropius founded his school of applied art called Bauhaus, where painters like Wassily Kandinsky and Paul Klee made important contributions. The instructors at the Bauhaus understood that in our time it was impossible to ignore the mass production of objects, even houses, and that they could and should guarantee, with appropriate designs, function and beauty. A discipline was thus born in Dessau which we now call industrial design, whereby even mass-produced objects were designed by choosing the most appropriate techniques and materials and by identifying shapes that were easy to reproduce and were sensible.

The same concepts when applied to architecture brought the use of prefabricated structures (carefully designed in the same way) and the estimation of their proper sizes in relation to the activities they would be used for, for example, in the case of a house. Applications of such principles were most important in the Bauhaus school buildings themselves and particularly in the houses set aside for the teachers, among them the director's house, which inspired the drawings on these pages. In the same way, one could construct a city district by keeping in mind traffic and the fact that people need to be near useful public services. Thus an architectural style that was just right for people came into existence, but because it opposed the beliefs of Nazism, the school in Dessau was closed and Gropius was forced to leave the country.

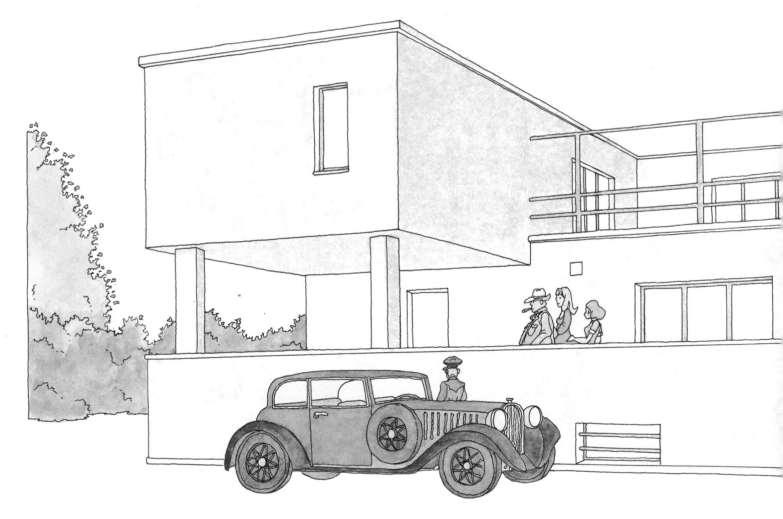

The house that Walter Gropius designed for himself and his family in 1925 is a perfect example of the adaptation of predetermined shapes (in this case cubes and parallelepipeds) to the needs of a rational use of space.

The second floor hangs over the first floor and forms a portico reached by a few steps; a large terrace leads to the second-floor living room.

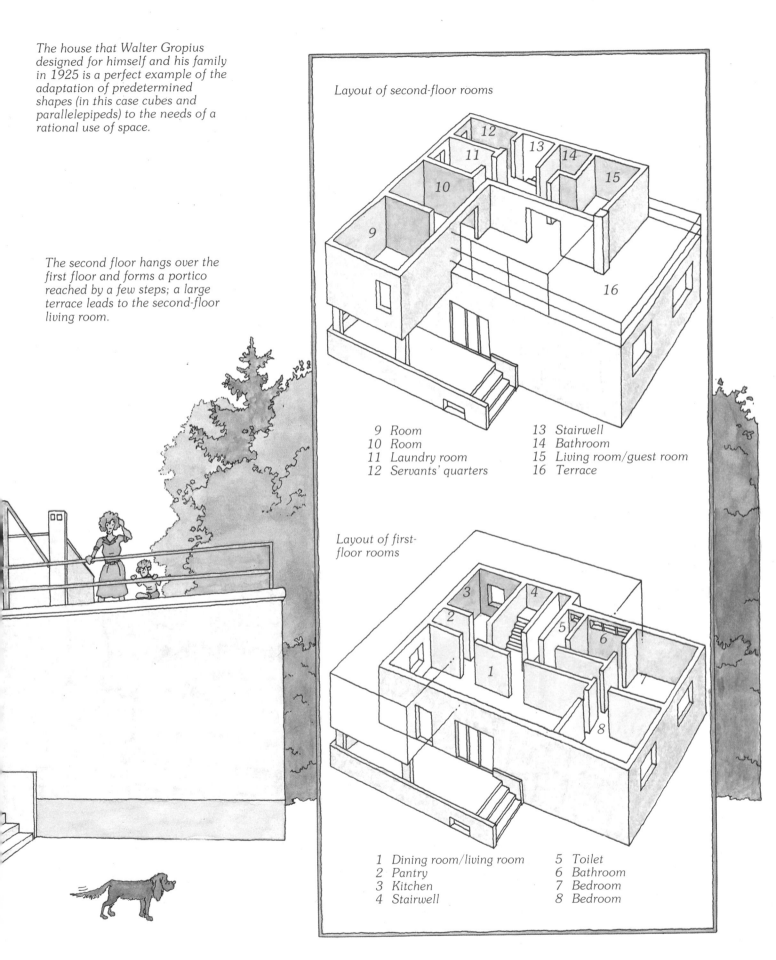

Layout of second-floor rooms

9   Room
10 Room
11 Laundry room
12 Servants' quarters
13 Stairwell
14 Bathroom
15 Living room/guest room
16 Terrace

Layout of first-floor rooms

1 Dining room/living room
2 Pantry
3 Kitchen
4 Stairwell
5 Toilet
6 Bathroom
7 Bedroom
8 Bedroom

53

BUILDING WITH REINFORCED CONCRETE

Pillars and beams of reinforced concrete are made by putting down a number of iron rods and pouring limestone around them in appropriate molds. They are very good at resisting contraction and contortion and are fairly flexible. In modern buildings only the backbone is made of reinforced concrete; between the pillars and beams are brick walls, usually hollow, because they are no longer required to resist compression. Floors are made of large hollow slabs of brick placed along the beams.

Water is essential for the preparation of limestone; the cement reacts with the water and hardens quickly, fixing the grains of sand.

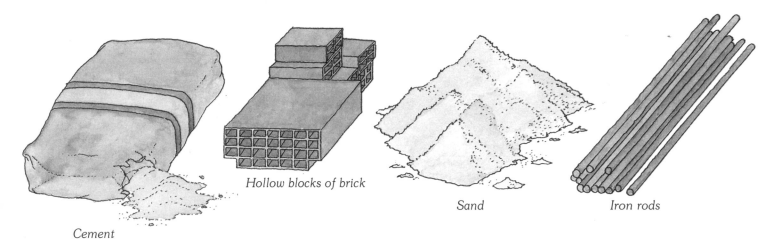

Cement

Hollow blocks of brick

Sand

Iron rods

To make a reinforced concrete building you first prepare scaffolding with planks or metal sheets on which the workers stand. The iron rods are immersed in the limestone mixture; reinforced cement beams are put down horizontally to make a floor, and hollow blocks of brick are placed between them.

Once the concrete casting is finished, the spaces between pillars are filled with hollow bricks or (especially for partition walls) prefabricated walls. In this construction phase you can start from the top or from the bottom.

A MODERN APARTMENT

Today buildings set aside for housing are often very large; they are always made of reinforced concrete and often have many different apartments, two or more on each floor.

The layout is always carefully designed and architects try to avoid unusable spaces; the entrance hall is often missing or is incorporated into the living room. The bedroom areas include bathrooms. The kitchen is often equipped with a breakfast table; here electrical appliances like washing machines, dishwashers, ovens, and stoves are placed near one another to form one unit.

These apartments often contain overhanging balconies, but sometimes, if the building is very tall, open galleries connect living rooms or other rooms by way of glass doors, with smaller galleries near the kitchen. Furniture is fairly sparse; most wardrobes are recessed into specially designed walls. Central heating can consist of traditional radiators or radiating panels placed inside the floor. In the empty space between the

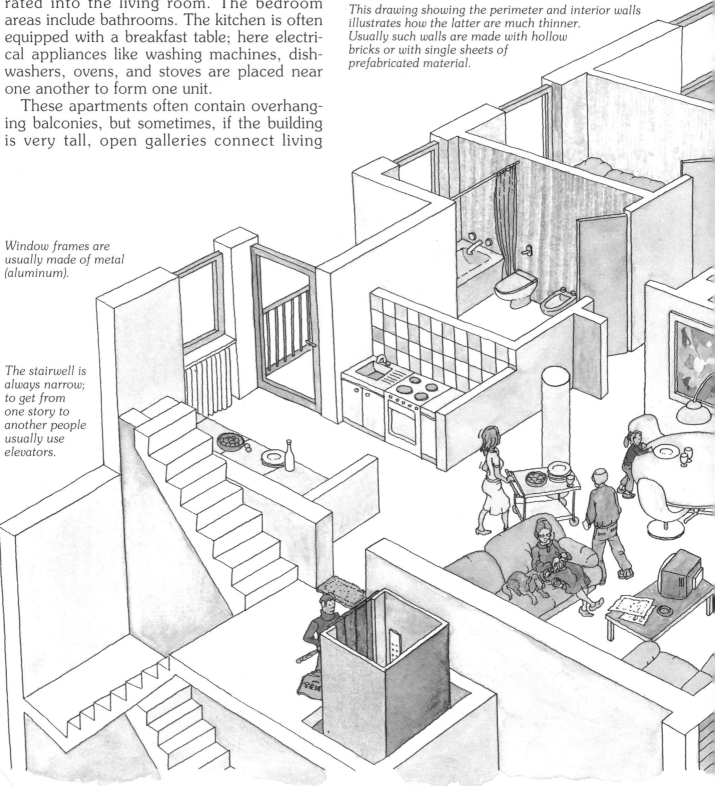

This drawing showing the perimeter and interior walls illustrates how the latter are much thinner. Usually such walls are made with hollow bricks or with single sheets of prefabricated material.

Window frames are usually made of metal (aluminum).

The stairwell is always narrow; to get from one story to another people usually use elevators.

walls are chimneys, water pipes, and electric wires. In addition to powering lightbulbs, electricity is used for kitchen appliances (mixers, toasters, waste disposals), boilers (if they don't run on gas), and other machines like stereos and televisions.

The elevator reaches the different floors in its own shaft; stairs are usually rather narrow, and for moving furniture people often use custom-built devices installed on the roof terrace of the building or mobile cranes brought by furniture movers.

Outside decorations can be made with strips of flat bricks similar to tiles that do not have a load-bearing function; sometimes cement tiles are used for decoration.

WATER IN THE HOME

The system of water distribution in a modern apartment is complicated. There are always two circuits: the inflow and the outflow. The inflow is divided into one branch for cold water and another branch that passes through a boiler for hot water; in the system illustrated here, the water is centralized in that it is heated in a boiler. The water comes out of taps because there is a certain amount of pressure. In the city, the communal water distribution system guarantees that there will be enough pressure to make water rise up to the fifth or sixth floor of a building. If the building is taller than that, a pump needs to be installed. The toilet, bath, and sink outflows end up directly in the sewers. The availability of water certainly improves the quality of life regarding hygiene. We should not, however, take advantage of it, because transporting water and purifying sewage require a lot of energy.

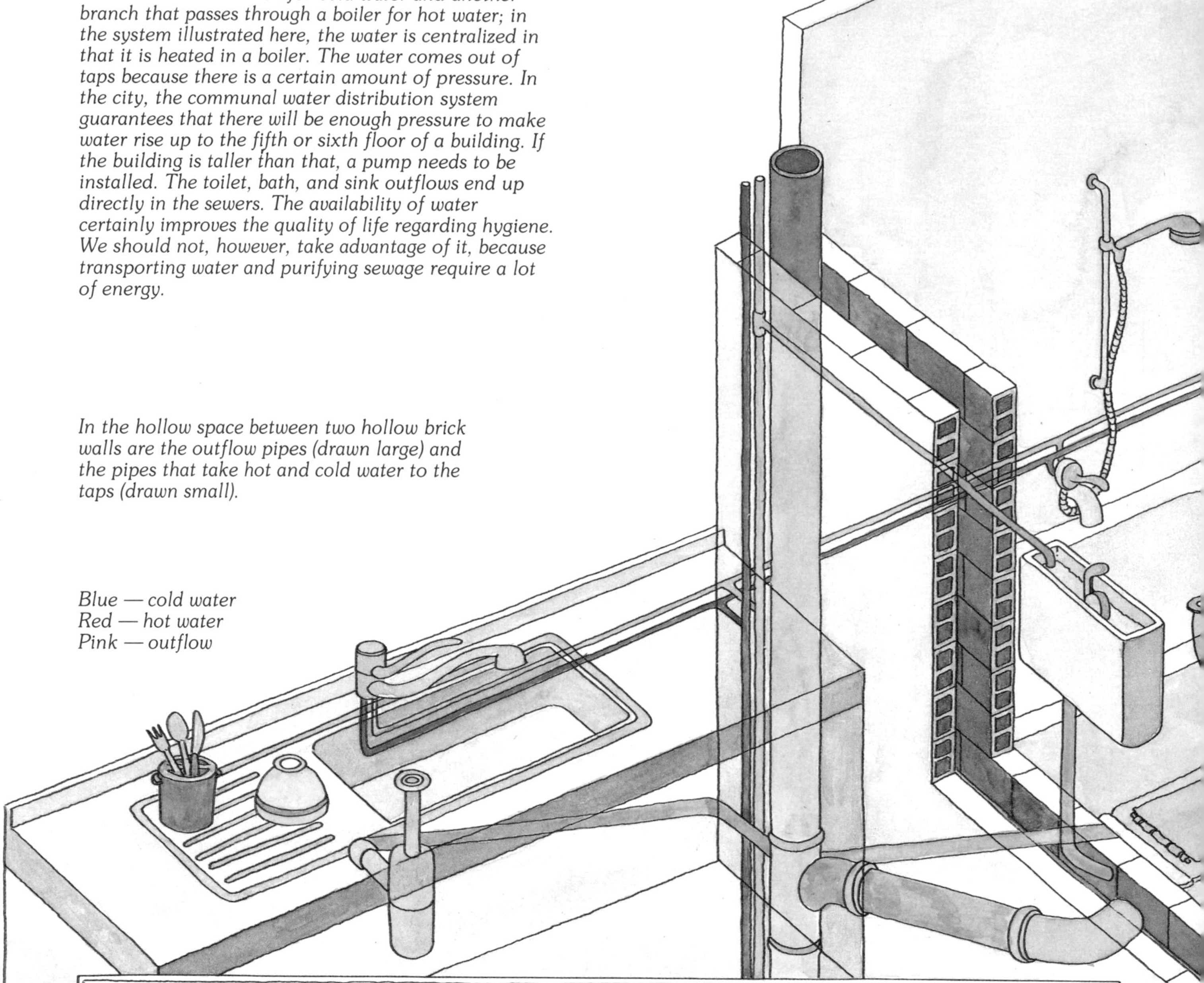

In the hollow space between two hollow brick walls are the outflow pipes (drawn large) and the pipes that take hot and cold water to the taps (drawn small).

Blue — cold water
Red — hot water
Pink — outflow

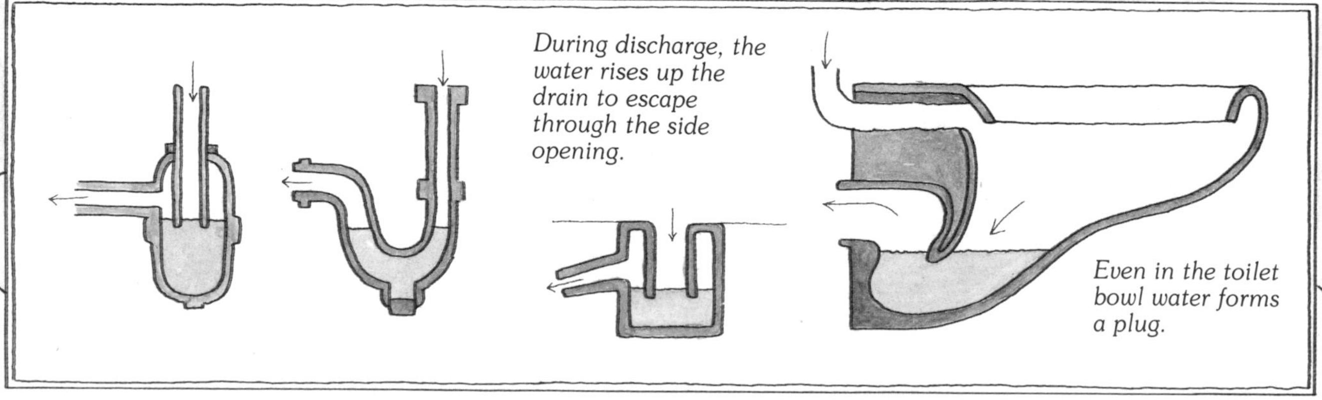

During discharge, the water rises up the drain to escape through the side opening.

Even in the toilet bowl water forms a plug.

To prevent lingering bad odors, water in the pipe acts as a valve and closes two branches of a **U** bend; this is a water plug.

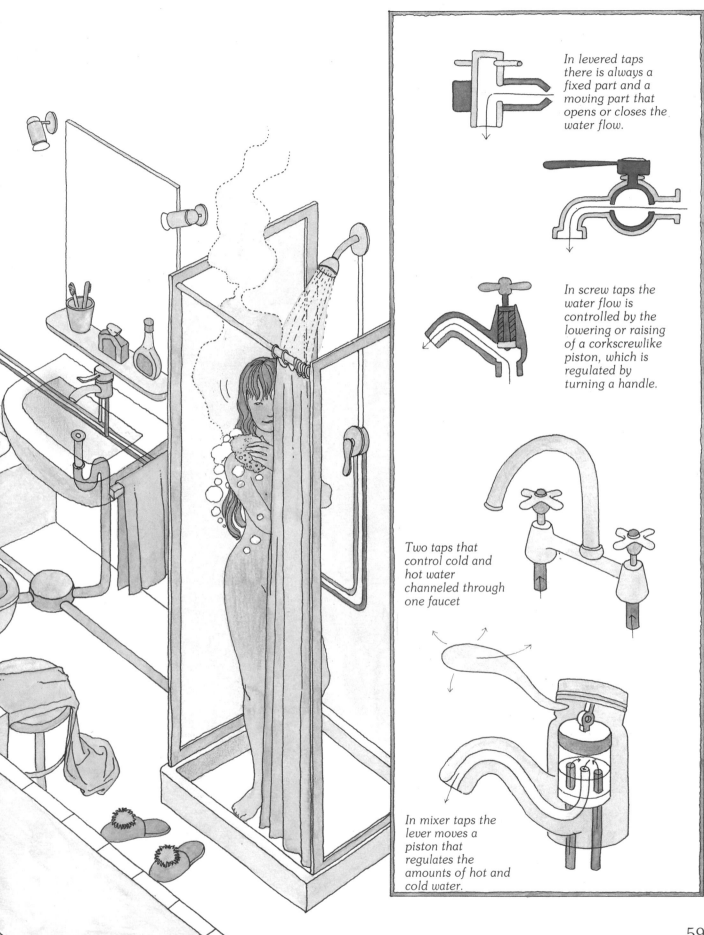

In levered taps there is always a fixed part and a moving part that opens or closes the water flow.

In screw taps the water flow is controlled by the lowering or raising of a corkscrewlike piston, which is regulated by turning a handle.

Two taps that control cold and hot water channeled through one faucet

In mixer taps the lever moves a piston that regulates the amounts of hot and cold water.

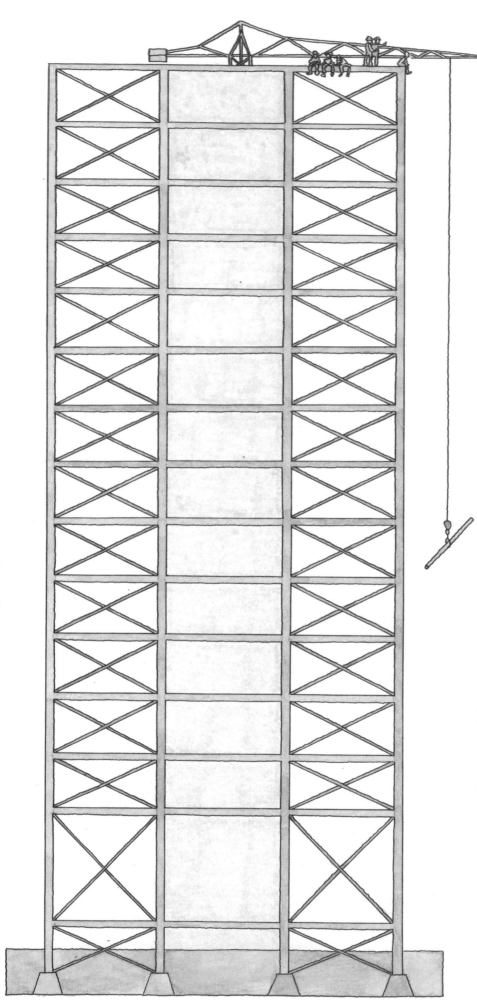

The shape of iron beams, a double **T**, allows the insertion of other pieces of brick, cement, or iron.

The metal structure is always made of a series of squares that are prevented from bending by rigid diagonal beams. We can see this arrangement of beams in the iron frameworks that support high-voltage electric cables or cranes. To build such metal castles the single pieces are lifted into position by cranes and hoists, then riveted together one by one; building an iron framework somewhat resembles opening a telescope.

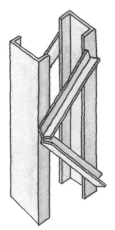

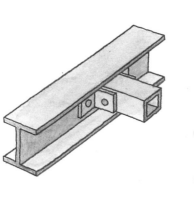

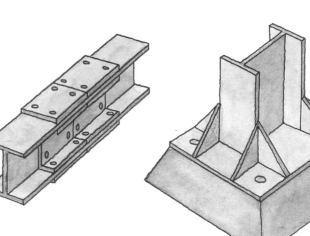

Some pillars are made of many pieces arranged in a **C**, bound together by angled pieces for greater strength.

The beams used to make the metal framework of a skyscraper are never solid, but are shaped like a double **T**; various sections are joined by riveting or welding plates.

At the base of pillars are elements that are made by various angled pieces that distribute the whole weight of the structure evenly over a large area.

BUILDING WITH IRON

Very tall buildings (buildings with more than thirty floors) can, if made of reinforced concrete, become too heavy. To support them, the foundations must be very large, with possible damage to the water table (the deposits of water that lie under the surface) and to manmade underground structures (like city underground trains, sewers, gas tunnels, or electricity tunnels). It was therefore necessary to reconsider iron structures and to use other construction materials as well. In a skyscraper there is always a large and light metal framework where, like in reinforced concrete buildings, prefabricated walls are placed between beams. Of course, such a construction system is very expensive and can be used only to make the most of building space. Once typical in only North American cities, skyscrapers are common today in other parts of the world as well.

GLOSSARY

Apse. See Transept.

Aqueduct. A system that carries water from a reservoir to the user. Roman aqueducts were overground structures consisting of a series of stone or brick arches that supported a canal rendered waterproof with mortar or sheets of lead. Many of these aqueducts are still in good condition. Today aqueducts are underground and made with piping, and they always consist of pumping stations that put pressure on water, allowing it to rise into hydraulic systems in buildings.

Arch. A curved architectural structure placed on two *piers*. Made of various materials (stone or brick), an arch is supported because each segment rests some of its weight on adjacent segments down to the piers. The highest part is called the keystone. To stop the pieces from falling during construction, an arch-shaped wooden structure is usually placed between the piers, and the various pieces are placed on top of it. The strength of the structure can be increased by inserting lime or cement between the segments. The two principal types of arch are distinguishable by their different curvatures—a round arch has a semicircular curve, and a pointed arch (typical of Gothic architecture) is formed by the intersection of two semicircles that meet in a point at the top.

Architrave. A horizontal beam that leans against two columns, pillars, or side posts.

Art nouveau. An architectural (and generally artistic) style that appeared in Belgium and spread to the rest of Europe between 1890 and the first decades of the 1900s. Typical of this style was the frequent use of curved and floral designs and the decorative and structural use of iron. It is known as art nouveau in Belgium and France, Liberty in Italy, Modern Style in England, Jugendstil in Germany, Sezessionstil in Austria, and Modernismo in Spain.

Attic. Any floor that serves as a ceiling for the floor below and as a floor for the story above. An attic is also an area under the roof, especially when it is reserved as a storage area.

Balustrade. A group of equally sized columns topped by a continuous architrave. It is used as a parapet or separation.

Baroque. An architectural (and generally artistic) style of the seventeenth and eighteenth centuries. Baroque elements in buildings, although not always with a load-bearing function, are not straight and often seem bizarre and showy. In France manifestations of baroque are named after the king of the time, as in Louis XIV, Louis XV, and occasionally Louis XVI.

Basalt. A volcanic rock that was often used as a building material. It can be polished with abrasives.

Beam. A construction element that is made of a tree trunk, an iron bar, or a concrete casting. When placed vertically it has a load-bearing function; placed horizontally, it supports low levels of flexion.

Brick. A construction material made with clay dried in the sun (in which case it is known by the Spanish word *adobe*) and eventually mixed with straw or with kiln-fired clay. It has an oblong shape. The fired bricks most often used today are hollow, that is, they have large cavities that lighten their weight, but only if they are not load-bearing (for example, in the construction of a partition).

Buttress. An architectural structure typical of Gothic style. It leans against a wall, opposing the horizontal stress that the wall is subject to, thanks to the weight of an overhead vault.

Carpentry. The activity of craftsmen (called carpenters) who work on the wooden structures of a building.

Casting. The pouring of *concrete* into appropriate containers (molds) from which, hardening, they take their shape.

Cement. A building material made of a mixture of minerals containing calcium oxide, iron, and various silicates, to which are added sand and gravel. With water, the cement reacts and binds, and with heat it hardens and contracts.

Central heating. A system for heating a building. Usually heated by gasfire, a boiler, a complex system of pipes, carries hot water to various floors where it circulates in the appropriate radiator. Water circulates because it rises when heated and falls when cold. This is usually assisted by a pump.

Ceramic. Produced by firing clay in kilns, ceramic is used for making containers, and if treated with special salts it can be covered with a glaze, in which case it is called majolica. Ceramic is also called terracotta.

Cistern. A container used to collect rainwater. In the past large cisterns were built underground.

Clay. Sedimentary rock, made mostly of silicate of magnesium or of aluminum, formed by the accumulation of sea or lake mud. When moist, it can be easily shaped by hand or with tools. When heated by the sun or in special ovens it becomes hard. An object made in this way is called ceramic or terracotta.

Column. A load-bearing architectural element. Usually a circular section, it can be made with various materials and always involves a base, the main part, called a shaft, and a capital placed above, upon which rests the *architrave*.

Concrete. A mixture made of a binding substance (cement or water lime) and inert substances such as sand, gravel, rubble, and water. It is filtered into a cavity in the form required (the mold). Hardening takes one to two hours, but the greatest resistance to compression occurs after a few months.

Cross vault. See Vault.

Cupola. A covering architectural structure, usually circular (very rarely elliptical or polygonal) and realized with a group of segments that make up a semispherical shape. It is usually topped by a *lantern* and sometimes by a spire.

Eclecticism. An architectural style common in the late 1800s and in the early 1900s, where a variety of past styles converge. One form of eclecticism is the late-nineteenth-century style called neo-Gothic, which repeated elements of Gothic.

Firebricks. A type of ceramic resistant to heat. Firebricks are used wherever there is a need to isolate heat.

Flight. The part of a stairway between two floors. To keep the area the stairs occupy narrower, two flights of stairs are incorporated between floors.

Fresco. A picture painted directly on the plaster of a wall. Usually artists sketched a picture (sinopite) with only one color; then, on a new and more delicate layer of fresh plaster, they would quickly complete the fresco. The pigment became incorporated into the plaster before it dried. The Romans made frescoes (encaustic paintings) by mixing colors in melted wax that was applied to the plaster.

Gothic. An architectural style present in Europe from the beginning of the twelfth century, characterized by the upward thrust of its buildings and the constant use of the *arch* and ogive vault.

Granite. Formed in the depths of the subsoil by the consolidation of magma, this rock can surface after the effects of erosion. Granite can also be formed by the transformation (metamorphosis) of rocks accumulated as sediment. Granite is used in building because of its solidity and because one can polish its surface with abrasives.

Hypocaust. The hot air chamber under a Roman bath.

Inert. Materials that, when mixed, have no binding function. For example, sand, gravel, and rubble in concrete are inert.

Iron beam. An iron element shaped in a way to increase its resistance to bending stress.

Lacunar ceiling. A hollow space, usually square, sunk into a ceiling.

Lantern. A structure placed on a *cupola*. It has openings that can be turned into windows, allowing light to reach the highest part of the cupola. Usually it has another smaller cupola on top.

Lime. A substance obtained by cooking limestone in specially made ovens. The chemical reaction created by treating the final product (caustic lime) with water produces slaked lime. Water lime is a mixture that can bind in humid places and even underwater.

Limestone. Sedimentary rock, 50 percent of which is made of calcium carbonate. Because it is soft, it can be easily shaped and was frequently used as a building material.

Mansard. A window that allows light into an area below the roof. The term comes from the French architect François Mansart (1598-1666). Usually, below the mansard, the angle of the roof is narrower to allow more interior space. Above the mansard the angle widens. Roofs with two angles are also called mansards. The term is also applied to rooms lit by this type of window.

Marble. A calcareous crystalline rock that is formed by a long process of transformation (metamorphosis). It can have various colors, often vivid, as well as veins.

Mezzanine. The floor of a building between the first floor and the second floor; often it has a low ceiling.

Mortar. A mixture of bonding substances (lime), sand, and water which hardens on contact with air. Largely used as a construction material, it is usually placed between bricks.

Nave. See Transept.

Neoclassical. An architectural and artistic style that in general imitated themes from classical Greek and Roman art owing to the influence of the works of Andrea Palladio (1508-1580); it is strongest in reaction to baroque and rococo in the second half of the eighteenth century and the first decades of the nineteenth century.

Overhang. A building's architectural component that juts out past the line of the wall.

Parastas. A pillar incorporated into a wall. If not load-bearing it is called a pilaster strip.

Pier. A vertical architectural element that holds up the *architrave*. It always comes in pairs. The *arch* is also held up by two piers.

Pilaster strip. A relief that juts out of a wall and has the appearance of a column or a pillar. Usually it is not load-bearing.

Pillar. A vertical architectural element that is load-bearing.

Plaster. A thin layer of mortar that is spread on a wall.

Porcelain. A ceramic obtained from clay which contains kaolin (an aluminum silicate that binds the mixture) and feldspar (an aluminum and potassium silicate that melts and forms a glassy mass). The word *porcelain* comes from the seashell fragments with which it was believed Chinese porcelains were made, described in the thirteenth century by Marco Polo. The word *kaolin* comes from the Chinese *Kao-ling* (meaning "skeleton," because it strengthens the product).

Rationalism. An architectural (and generally artistic) trend that originated in the arts and crafts school called Bauhaus, founded in 1919 in Dessau (Saxony) by the architect Walter Gropius (1883-1969). Typical of rationalism was the desire to design structures and architectural elements that would in the most practical and efficient manner complete the function for which they were meant and that would help facilitate the mass production of such elements. In the case of houses, rationalism proposed building with prefabricated structures that can be put together according to a planned urban layout.

Renaissance. An architectural (and generally artistic) style that spread through Europe in the 1400s and 1500s, taking its cue from the revaluation of man's position at the center of the world (called Humanism) and reviving elements of Roman architecture. A late manifestation of the Renaissance is called Mannerism, and it includes the paintings of Michelangelo Buonarroti (1475-1564) and the architectural work of Giorgio Vasari (1511-1574). Later it evolved into baroque. The High Renaissance works of Andrea Palladio evolved into neoclassical style at the end of the 1700s.

Rococo. An architectural and decorative style that in the beginning of the 1700s became part of the complex and desirable style called *baroque.*

Romanesque. An architectural style in Europe between the tenth and twelfth centuries in which the rounded arch is prevalent.

Roof. The upper covering of a building. It can come in various forms: with one slope (made of only one inclined plain), two inclined surfaces, a cupola, or a mansard roof. A beam that in traditional construction was made of wood connects each supporting truss to the next. A roof is covered with tiles, made of slate, metal, or as in many typical farmhouses thatch.

Round arch. See Arch.

Side post. Vertical elements in a building that mark the edges of a door or window.

Stave. Each of the wooden elements that constitute the side of a barrel. The term is also applied to the flat traves or beams used for the adornment or the construction of timber floors.

Stucco. An elastic material made of mortar and marble dust that when hardened looks like marble. Easily shaped, it was long used in decorations, sometimes with repeating motifs, depending on the method of molding it.

Terracotta. A synonym for ceramic.

Tile-lintel floor. A ceramic construction element, generally hollow, that is partly inserted into and leaned on a framework of reinforced concrete beams to make a supported floor. Smaller flat tiles are used to make weak ceilings.

Tiles. Ceramic pieces used to cover a roof. There are cupped tiles, which are semicylindrical, similar to fingernails, and flat tiles that are hooked by overlapping them, thanks to upturned edges.

Transept. A church usually has two naves (named after the Latin *nave* because they are shaped like a ship's keel); the main nave runs from the entrance to the altar and to the apse, and the other runs across at a right angle to the first. The intersection of the two is called the transept.

Truss. An architectural structure usually made of wood (and sometimes iron) which supports the roof. It is in the shape of an isosceles triangle or a very wide **A**. A roof's framework is always made of many trusses.

Tympanum. A large triangular (isosceles) architectural element that is placed vertically on top of the *architrave* in ancient classical temples.

U bend. In sanitary systems, a **U**-shaped pipe that always remains full of water (because of a law of physics) and stops bad smells from going up the outflow pipes.

Vault. An architectural structure that covers a building. Usually the vault rests on *piers* or large columns. The inside has a concave surface (intrados) and the outside a convex surface (extrados). Among the most common forms are a barrel vault, a typically Roman semicircular vault; a pointed Gothic vault; an annular vault, in the shape of a semicircular ring; a pendant vault shaped like an inflated ship's sail; and a cross vault, made by the right-angle intersection of two barrel vaults, which in a church hang over the area where the main nave crosses the transept.